Niu Voices

Niu Voices:
Contemporary Pacific Fiction 1

HUIA

First published in 2006 by Huia Publishers
39 Pipitea Street, P O Box 17-335
Wellington, Aotearoa New Zealand
www.huia.co.nz

ISBN 1-86969-254-3

Cover Artwork: Sheyne Tuffery

National Library of New Zealand Cataloguing-in-Publication Data
Niu voices.
(Contemporary Pacific fiction ; 1)
ISBN 1-869692-54-3
1. Short stories, New Zealand. 2. New Zealand poetry—21st
century. 3. Pacific Island fiction (English) 4. Pacific Island poetry
(English) I. Series.
NZ820.8—dc 22

Published with the support of the Pacific Arts Committee of Creative New Zealand

ARTS COUNCIL OF NEW ZEALAND *TOI AOTEAROA*

Contents

Foreword

'The word "niu" has two meanings in Pacific languages. It most commonly refers to the coconut, the ancient and enduring tree of life in most island environments, but in the pidgin "niu" also means "new", "novel" or "different". It is with this complex and perhaps contradictory combination of both ancient and the new – the "niu" – that I wonder about future directions for Pacific art.'

Teresia Teaiwa, Senior Lecturer and Programme Director, Pacific Studies, Victoria University of Wellington, in *Loop Magazine*, Sept/Nov 2000

The journey of *Niu Voices* started in 2003 with a series of workshops held in Auckland, Wellington and Christchurch. Initiated by the Pacific Arts Committee of Creative New Zealand, each workshop offered creative writing skills, advice on applying for funding, how to get work published and where to go for support. An informal network of emerging Pacific writers around the country was also established.

Sixty-five writers attended these workshops, which culminated in the publication of *First Draft: a collection of work by emerging Pacific writers.* For many of these writers, this was the first time they had had their work published. It was also the first time they had attended a writing workshop.

A follow-up Pacific writers' workshop called *Second Draft* was held at Auckland University of Technology in Auckland in 2005. This provided an opportunity for participants to build on their previous workshop experience, and from this forum, the need for *Niu Voices* emerged.

Niu Voices offers writers of Pacific heritage the chance to have their work read by a wider audience. They come from a diverse range of backgrounds, styles and experiences, and this is reflected in their work.

The future direction of Pacific art lies in the words, the ideas and creative expressions of Pacific peoples. This publication can act as a marker in the journey towards the discovery of new Pacific voices within Aotearoa, Niu Sila, New Zealand.

I would like to offer special thanks to the original workshop facilitators Adrienne Jansen and Professor Albert Wendt; the Pacific Arts Committee members (past and present); Huia Publishers (Robyn, Brian and Renee); *Spasifik* magazine (Innes Logan); Auckland University of Technology (Isabella Rasch); and Nectar Design Ltd (www.nektar.co.nz). Thanks also to Selina Tusitala Marsh for editing *Niu Voices*.

Anton Carter
Arts Adviser, Pacific Islands Arts
Creative New Zealand
September 2006

Felicia

Taria Baquié

Felicia said her mum had gone and sworn offa men for good cos they're not nothing but a fat waste of space. Anyway, her mum had said most of them weren't even good for the one thing she was sure God had put them on the earth for. I asked her what that was cos I was too dumb to know God's plan for the men on the earth, and she looked at me funny like she had some big secret that I didn't know nothing 'bout, and she was trying to eye me up to see if I was worth knowing it too. For giving the pleasure, she told me. I still wasn't sure what she meant by the pleasure, but I didn't really want to, especially from someone like Felicia who always had stains on her T-shirts and never brushed her hair once.

Anyway, Felicia told me her mum had said that all she ever needed was Felicia and never mind any rotten old dog that tries to woo her just for some cash and pleasure. I could tell by the way she was looking at me that she was showing off how much her mum loved her that she would even sacrifice getting herself a husband. And she said that probably my mum wishes my daddy wasn't round too, wasting space and being a pain in the bum. Well, when she said that, I decided that I'd had enough of smelly Felicia from number 14 telling me my daddy wasn't good for nothing, so I ran home to tell.

Felicia's house wasn't quite opposite mine, but it was next to Mr Fatialofa's house, which was. We all lived in a dead end, and hardly any cars drove down there, so I could ride my bike wherever I wanted. My driveway even sloped downwards, so once you got to the bottom, you were going fast enough to get a bit of wind on your face, and you could ride all the way up to Mr Fatialofa's front lawn without your feet touching the pedals.

Sometimes Felicia would be out too, watching from her driveway or sitting on her fence. Most of the time she just watched me with her small eyes and sniffy nose. She'd say, nah, you're just a baby. I don't even wanna play your stink baby games, even though she was only eleven, and I was seven-almost-eight. Also, she liked watching her American movies, and she always talked 'bout Julia Roberts like they were sisters, and she even said she was American like Julia even though she talked like a bunga. I could tell she was a bunga anyway cos she had her brown skin like the rest of us and her flat nose and big dirty feet with no shoes on. I pretended to believe her though just so she didn't feel bad for lying. I didn't know where her daddy was who should have told her not to lie. Or where her mummy was either cos I had never seen her come out of her house. I didn't even know what she looked like, but I figured that she was beautiful-looking if she could turn away men like Felicia said she did. But all she needs is me, Felicia would say. Just me.

I was out riding one day, listening to the whirring of the bike wheels as they spun round and round and feeling the pedals' bumpy plastic on my bare feet. Felicia came over to me as I stopped to rest. First she had kinda stood away a while like she normally did, like she was waiting for me to do something. I didn't want to talk to Felicia that day cos I knew all she was going to do was tell me my bike was dumb, even when she didn't even have one. She always shouted at me as I whizzed past her sitting on the fence, her bum spread out under her like a hamburger patty, that her mum had bought her a cooler bike for Christmas once. Except someone stole that bike and no wonder too cos it was a flash one. It would make your bike look like a tin can if you put it next to my bike my mum got me, which would be like a Lamborghini. Anyway, I kept pretending not to see her standing by the lamp-post. She must have had enough after a while though cos I stopped for a rest, and she came over to me.

Up close, Felicia looked like she had never had a bath before. Her hair was all frizzy, and she still had bits of dried stuff in the corner of her eye. When she opened her mouth to talk to me, I could see her yellow teeth, but I tried not to look too hard in case she noticed and said something mean 'bout my face to make up for me staring at her yellow teeth. So I had to look at the gap between her eyebrows cos it seemed like just 'bout the only place that wasn't covered in something that shouldn't have been there. You can play at my house, she said. I didn't really want to go play at her house, but my mum always said that if someone offers you something of theirs you'd better take it so as not to give offence. I didn't know much 'bout giving Felicia any offence, but I knew that if I said no she might give me a thump, seeing as she was older and bigger than me. Okay, I said, and I followed behind her, wheeling my bike beside me as I tried to step on my own shadow so I didn't burn my feet. I left my bike out on her front lawn and followed her inside.

Her house had as much light as the inside of a shoe and smelt almost the same. I don't know why they had all their curtains shut cos it trapped the flies in and kept the sun out. She showed me her room and said her mum was sleeping next door. It was dark in her room too, but I could see all the stuff on her floor like bits of paper and toys, which all looked like she'd found somewhere and didn't get any of them new from the shop. Everything was on the floor but not this plastic man with a beard who stood on her window sill. She said he was Jesus who was coming to save us cos her Nana said he was, and if you pray to him, he'll give you things. I thought then maybe Felicia should pray more to get some new stuff, but then I never prayed and didn't even know that was Jesus by her bed, and I had a bike, tin can or not.

Anyway, she said did I want some peanuts, but I wondered if her peanuts were old cos it didn't look like anything in her house was new, but I said yes please cos I didn't want to give her any offence. We went out to the lounge, and I waited while she went to the kitchen to get the peanuts. When she came back she gave me five peanuts exactly and kept the rest for herself. She turned the TV on and just sat right up close to it so all I could see was the back of her scruffy head, and she even had the volume up real loud though I thought her mum was supposed to be sleeping.

Now, I wish that I'd reminded her 'bout her mum in the next room, but at the time I was busy trying not to touch anything and trying to slip those five peanuts into my pocket so I didn't have to eat them. Well, Felicia was right up to the TV, and I was just standing behind her when her mum came storming into the lounge and gave me such a fright that I jumped, even though I wasn't doing anything bad.

Felicia's mum was real angry and told Felicia to turn that goddam TV off. I was glad she didn't notice me standing there, but soon enough she looked up and saw me. Felicia's mum didn't look much like Felicia cos she was real skinny, but she had scraggly hair and was wearing a dirty white T-shirt, and as she yelled and pointed, I could see her boobs moving round like she wasn't even wearing a bra. I didn't think anyone could be so angry at me for doing nothing. I wasn't even sitting on her dirty sofa, but she was yelling at me anyway, and I hoped she didn't want to check my pockets and find the peanuts and take the offence. She was yelling at me to get the eff outta her house, and who the eff was I in her goddam house, and Felicia get her the eff outta here. Spit was coming out of her mouth as she yelled, and I was so scared she was gonna give me a hiding I just ran out of there with Felicia just staring at the TV like she was off on another planet. I hoped, as I ran past Felicia's mum, that she wouldn't try to stop me or anything, but she was too busy swearing and pointing and jiggling her boobs around. I didn't stop running till I got home, but I made sure to get my bike in case Felicia never gave it back.

I hardly ever saw Felicia after that cos we moved not long after. But that was the first and last time I ever saw Felicia's mum, who didn't seem that beautiful to me. And no matter what Felicia had said 'bout her mum who only needed her, I couldn't imagine her mum with the stained clothes ever saying anything nice to Felicia, or to anyone. I don't think you could live in the dark and forget 'bout your daughter and be nice at the same time. No wonder Felicia told me lies 'bout her mum and who cares 'bout no daddy being a waste of space.

Anyway, I guess there's no harm in pretending to be someone you weren't, especially if you had to be Felicia.

Papa

Taria Baquié

My papa was up in the hospital ready to pass away, and my cousin was being mean to me. She was telling me I ain't gonna be nofing the way I always carried on like a bloody retarded handi, but I thought she must have been the bloody retarded handi if she didn't even know you're supposed to call them disabled. I thought if I had one of those wheelchairs like some disableds do then I'd run it right over her big toes and then chase her out of the hospital. And didn't she even care with Papa lying on that bed all pale and skinny with those tubes coming out of his arms and those things next to his bed and Mama sitting there holding onto his hand as if he was gonna run away? And then I had my mum tell me can't I even let her dad pass in peace? Just cos she'd walked in right when I reached over to pull Joanne's hair, even though she'd just called me a gollywog, and never mind what Joanne was saying, you don't cause a fuss in the hospital with all those nice nurses around and your papa lying there waiting for the gates of St Peter to buzz him in. I thought nurses or no nurses, if Joanne called me gollywog again, it'd be her seeing St Peter way before my papa.

I don't know why my mum didn't just say Papa was dying. She always said, oh, Mere, Papa's passing; he's going to pass soon, Mere. Passing reminded me of the way my dad would yell at the TV, pass the ball! Pass the ball! And he'd get up on his big feet and stomp around and wave his arms in the air and yell, pass it!, then, oh, you bloody idiot! when the guy kept the ball to himself. I said to my mum why didn't she just say Papa was dying and not this passing thing, which sounded like he was playing rugby when he hadn't even played since he was a boy. And she would sigh and frown like I asked her a hard question or something and just tell me it was nicer that way, Mere. It's just nicer, you know? And I'd have to say yes, even though I didn't really know, but if I said that then she'd get tears in her eyes and ask Jesus for strength and tell me I was trying. You can be *trying* sometimes, Mere, she'd say. I just find you *trying*, but that don't mean I don't love you, so go brush your teeth and don't you worry 'bout Papa. You just worry 'bout what you're getting in your sandwiches tomorrow, okay?

I told her never mind 'bout no stinky sandwiches. I swapped them with William Falatoa, anyway, cos his mum gives him dry noodle cakes, but if she stopped treating me like a baby maybe I wouldn't *try* so much. I said try the way she did, all long and drawn out, which is how I knew she meant it in a bad way. And my mum would say what's William Falatoa's mum doing giving him dry noodle cakes for lunch? That's no way to feed a growing boy. She seemed to have forgotten that he didn't eat the dry noodle cakes. I ate them, and he got my jam-on-white-bread sandwiches with the crusts cut off. Anyway, with my papa on the brink of passing in the hospital and poor William Falatoa with the dry noodle cakes, she'd forgotten 'bout me telling her I wasn't no baby any more, and why couldn't she just say Papa's gonna die, not he's passing soon like he was Jonah Lomu.

Anyway, even though my mum told me don't be surprised, Mere, when he passes, it's been such a long, hard battle, I said I wasn't gonna be surprised. He'd been in hospital for ages now, and once he told me he was gonna die cos he was old and tired and Mama kept giving him a hard time. He told me, I been through a few things in my years, Mere, but, you know, it's that grandma of yours that's going to put the final nail in my coffin with all that growling she does. I told him didn't I already know 'bout it with my mum, and she's probably gonna put the final nail in my coffin too, and he laughed till his eyes watered, and he couldn't breathe proper.

I spent lots of time with Papa up in that hospital cos he said there was nothing to do but look at the wall and piss in his bottle. I use to be the most important man in the village, he'd say, and now they make me piss in a bottle! Like I was a baby! And aue, the food here, Mere. It's not food. We feed the pigs back home better stuff than this!

Sometimes if I had some money, I ran down to the McDonalds near the hospital and bought Papa a Big Mac, even though he wasn't allowed one, so we had to hide it from Mum. Sometimes though, Mum would come in, and he'd still have crumbs on his face, and she'd say, don't you know, Dad, that your heart is in trouble, and do you think you should be clogging your arteries with that fatty burger? And Mere, you should know better! And where'd you get your money from, ah? And then she'd say had I forgotten Papa was on the brink of passing, and did I want to send him over the edge early?

I always thought the way she carried on 'bout St Peter and those big white gates that shouldn't she be pleased for Papa going to a nicer place than this boring hospital where they make him piss in a bottle when he use to be the most important man in the village, and why not meet that St Peter with the sweet taste of a cheesy beef patty with lettuce and extra mayo still in his mouth? No, there's no better place than God's Kingdom, but that don't mean, Mere, that you can start digging his grave now. You should know better. And then she'd sigh and frown, and I figured that meant I was being trying.

Papa told me that my mum always took life too seriously, and it's hard to get a good laugh out of her when she's always worrying 'bout everything. Like, Mere, are your socks matching and is your hair brushed? And you'd better pray that's not a tattoo on your arm, but it is a tattoo cos I put it there, and it's not even a real one, but she doesn't care. She says it makes me look like a rough-necked gangster like my uncle, and no child of mine is getting tangled up in no gangster rubbish, so you go wash it off. Papa said to never mind 'bout the way she carries on; she just loves me and wants the best, and I should listen to her cos she knows more than me cos she's been around longer.

I started thinking maybe I should listen to her and try not to be so trying, and Mama, who would be sitting by Papa's bed holding his hand, would say listen to your mother, Mere, listen to your mother. Even when I tried to explain that I do listen I just didn't understand what she meant sometimes, she would still just hold Papa's hand and say, listen to your mother, listen to your mother. When I was your age, Mere, and I didn't listen to my mother, she would get very angry and say to me to get the stick outside and pah! I'd get the hiding for not listening to my mother when she say to me to peel the taro and stop talking to that boy. Lucky your mum don't take the stick to you. I still got the lines on my bum.

And then Papa would laugh like he was remembering something, like maybe he was the boy that Mama got the stick for, and Mama would look at him and tell him what's funny. You just lie there and behave. Papa would smile then and say, aue, Mummy, and wink at me. Then I'd know that's what he meant by the hammering of that nail into his coffin, but even then he still held her hand, and she still had his lines on her bum.

That day Joanne called me gollywog was the same day Papa died. I had to stay at the hospital with Papa and Joanne cos my mum had gone to drop Mama off at home to eat some KFC for dinner. Mama wasn't allowed to eat the KFC at the hospital cos then Papa would scab some, and he had the clogged arteries and was only allowed mushy broccoli, and Joanne would scab too, and she had the fat legs and shouldn't have been allowed anything till she could start walking proper and not waddle like a penguin.

Anyway, with my mum gone again, Joanne started to be mean some more, wiggling her one big caterpillar eyebrow as she laughed at me. Shame, she said. You got in trouble again for causing a fuss. Fa, you're always getting in trouble, Mere. You're stink to your mum. See what I told you 'bout being a handi? And Aunty told me you're always giving him Big Macs and trying to send him over early. You're sad, Mere. Why you wanna kill Papa for, giving him those burgers? And then I had to say that she was just angry cos that meant there was less burgers for her fat bum to eat. I went to go lie on Papa's bed after that cos I knew Joanne would hit me cos she hated being called fat.

Papa was just lying there on those white sheets that had HOSPITAL printed across them in big blue letters, just in case you forgot where you were. When Mum came back he was just staring at the ceiling like he was trying to see through it or something. Mum just stood by the window, and no one said anything for ages, until Mum started looking down on the road and began complaining 'bout the cars and the smog, and God forbid the heavens opening up now. The only car park I could find was miles away and I don't got a brolly.

Where's Mama? Papa asked, and Mum came over from the window to tell him she was home having some dinner. She'd already told him before they left, but Papa forgot things easy. Mmm … kai, he said and closed his eyes. I just thought he'd fallen asleep, and I was waiting for his mouth to fall open like it normally does, and Mum would say, oh, he's trying to catch flies again, and the drool would run down his chin and into her tissue. But he just lay there, and I suppose that's when he died cos he didn't ever wake up again. Mum must've known too cos she got wet eyes and sat on the bed and started saying the Lord's Prayer, Our Father, who art in Heaven, even though she meant God, not her real father that just passed away.

I didn't even cry or nothing. I don't know why, but I was just thinking 'bout how that's probably the last time Mama will have KFC cos she'll want to go back to the Islands with Papa's body, and they don't got no KFC back there. No KFC and no McDonalds, and maybe they should send Joanne there. Then I'd have no more fat cousin with one eyebrow calling me gollywog. But now I've got no Papa cos he's dead and gone, but at least he doesn't have to piss into a bottle anymore. Mum told me, don't worry, Mere, it wasn't you with the Big Macs, so don't you go feeling bad. It was his time to go cos God wanted to see him. I couldn't be bothered saying I already know it wasn't those Big Macs cos he only ever had four, and Dad had eaten way more than that, and he was still allowed to piss in the toilet. And I knew it wasn't Mama either with her nagging and her hammering away on that nail. Papa had already told me ages ago he was old and tired, and nothing lasted forever. I'd said, even Joanne being mean to me and Mum treating me like a baby? And he just smiled and said, aue, Mere, aue.

Fugue (Extract)

An Apocalyptic Supernatural Thriller

Philip Siataga

Fugue 2 *Psychol.* loss of awareness of one's identity, often coupled with the flight from one's usual environment. *Oxford Dictionary*

Dissociative Fugue is characterised by sudden, unexpected travel away from home or one's customary place of work, accompanied by an inability to recall one's past and confusion about personal identity or the assumption of a new identity. *DSM IV Dissociative Disorders*

Part One

Like the imperceptible breaking of stem from limb
the last leaf falls,
trembling like the frail grasp of a memory passing.

Chapter One

10.30 p.m. University of Otago Library

The fluttering wings of a fantail, feathers shimmering silver in the evening light, captured Monique's gaze. Distracted from study, she watched through the wall-length window, as it darted and swerved with an effortlessness that breathed melodically across her retiring mind. She had been perched in her favourite study cubicle, shrouded in books and scribbled notes with a packet of salt and vinegar chips, for several hours. A self-absorbed smile creased her face as the last snack dissolved stealthily in her mouth. This had been her ritual for the last three years, a mock communion to the austere patron saint of libraries, whoever that might be. She shuffled her chair backwards, stretched her wings, flapped her hands, which were stiff from writing and head resting, and rose to leave.

The library was still full of students, most showing the familiar signs of mental fatigue; concentrated brows, vacant staring eyes, elongated yawns, amidst stilted conversations and whispered sweet nothings. She turned, momentarily, to see several of the books she had left sprawled across the wooden desk being shuffled unceremoniously onto a trolley by a gangly dreaded-haired Rastafarian. She took a quick glance at her notes; the cryptic translation of the enigmatic fragment invited a final curiosity. If it wasn't a recent find, why had it been withheld from the public for so long?

The *Wall Street Journal* report claimed the fragment was part of the most complete manuscript of the Dead Sea Scrolls in existence. The discovery of the ancient scrolls in eleven caves along the north-west shore of the Dead Sea shortly after World War Two had excited historians and archaeologists alike, particularly religious scholars hungry for new insights into a world over two millenniums past. For decades, speculations as to their meaning and current significance had simmered ceaselessly among scholars, religious zealots, conservative and liberal theologians, with only a select few having full access to the papyrus and animal-skin writings for several decades. In the past two years, more fragments had been emerging and finding a ready market, legal or not, to trade in.

As early as 1954, some fragments had appeared for sale in America without success. Over half a century later, the *Wall Street Journal* was repeating history. The latest scroll was up for sale. At ten metres long it was the lengthiest yet known. The report could not confirm whether it was a recent find or one that had remained 'hidden' since the scrolls were first discovered. To tempt would-be buyers, a fragment had already been authenticated by a small group of credible scholars but had not been confirmed by Israel's Antiquities Authority (IAA), the government agency in charge of archeological digs and artifacts. According to the report, the IAA was now investigating the claim and would bring charges against anyone selling or buying what it considered national property. The alleged cloak and dagger theories currently circling reminded her that, for some people, the obsession with artifacts of religious significance was not unlike the gravedigger mentality that had existed as long as there was something of value to bury.

Despite the publication of some photos by the *Biblical Archaeological Society* in November 1991 and the Huntington Library pledge to open their microfilm files of all the scroll photographs, few attempts to translate the manuscripts for the general public's consumption had popularised the documents enough for them to become mainstream. In general, it was not surprising that the public remained uninformed of their significance, and Monique had discovered that her own fascination with the subject was a luxury best kept for the tutorials where there was at least a modicum of value placed on its discussion.

A year earlier, Monique had intended to visit the caves near the ancient ruins of Qumran, some thirteen miles east of Jerusalem, as part of her OE, but had cancelled the guided tour at the last minute to tend to her father's needs. He had been a minister of religion with an infectious curiosity about things ancient. For reasons she could not fathom, God had decided that his demise would begin with renal failure, a result of diabetes and other complications. Morphine had relieved the pain but hastened the dying process, and it was a small joy that in his more lucid moments he was still able to conjure up some unanswered questions relating to biblical exegesis.

Monique loved the way he lit up when he understood a new term, or the lengths he went to in search of the essential meaning of a text. Even when she was a child, he delighted to sit her on his lap and tell her the Hebrew, the Aramaic or the Greek meaning of a particular word or phrase, perhaps because his curiosity was not shared deeply by most of the congregation or, more so she surmised, because he just wanted her to know something special. She often wondered what the Samoan equivalent was and now regretted her grasp of the native language of her parents was not fluent, not even close. She had discovered however, a new doubt previously unattended in her own religious convictions – why did he have to suffer?

As the youngest of four children, she would soak in the attention given to her by her father and dutifully attend to the religious duties he demanded. Only now, in her early twenties, did the student lifestyle present choices that were difficult to accommodate with her upbringing, including an increasing fondness for wine readily supplied by her two mischievous flatmates. Jessica Summer and Tavita Jones (her would-be boyfriend – if he wasn't so flippant and a sporting fanatic) were chalk and cheese but shared a dry sense of humour that lightened her more serious moments.

Monique's interest with the past was something her friends thought of as an endearing peculiarity, but they would politely dismiss conversation that headed enthusiastically down that road. She missed the lively, if not somewhat formal, conversations with her father that allowed her to talk and debate as if they were friends. But there was always a distance, a longing to understand him in a way that surpassed her status as a daughter. How interested he would have been if he could have read what she was now committing to memory. It had a familiar prophetic and apocalyptic ring and certainly wasn't any less weird than other, better-known texts. She mouthed the words quietly to herself.

> *It will come like a vulture's shadow shrouding the carcass of our history.*
> *It will devour the flesh of our memories.*
> *And brother will be as stranger and neighbour as ghost*
> *For all will call for mercy, but only a few will remember the places where it dwells.*

She slipped the photocopy of the fragment into her tapa-patterned satchel and fumbled for a CD-ROM. Feeling only tissues sent an involuntarily shiver spidering across her back. Panic was not something Monique experienced often. She prided herself on her relaxed manner and had a reputation among friends as the quintessential queen of mellowness. But tonight, as the florescent lights chased geometric shadows into the nooks and crannies of a battalion of book shelves, latent anxiety flowed. A moment later, she was in full flight, rushing past book stands, diving between empty rows, down the first flight of stairs and dashing through the library foyer.

Outside the library, the cool air and soft glow of street lights attempted to pacify her. To the left, leaves rustled on a row of cherry blossom trees spread uniformly along the walkway between the library and student cafeteria. She slowed, walking robotically along the concrete pavement, taking solitary and deliberate steps, which dulled the echo of the student horde that had flurried over it earlier that day. 'Where on God's green earth did I leave it?' Her breathing relaxed. She methodically retraced her steps, winding back the day, as a montage of activity flashed by: lectures dutifully attended, a hurried lunch, a spilled flat white in the Union Hall, an odd meeting with Jessica and – 'Aaaaargh,' she screamed. For the second time that night, spindly legs clambered over her. A hand flew from her shoulder followed by a startled but familiar voice.

'Whoa? What's up?' Tavita dropped his arm tentatively around her shoulders, uncertain whether to laugh or console. 'Shite-shite-shite-shite.' Monique breathed, slowly recollecting herself. He chose the latter. 'Want to come home?' he asked. She nodded, her mind reeling from the displacement of the CD-ROM and an intuition that it mattered a lot more than it should. Behind the posters and student notices clinging uniformly to the glass library doors, a silent observer followed their movements. Placing a finger-sized digital camera into his jacket pocket, he strode through the foyer doors, turned right and hurried away.

1.30 a.m. Turning the key in the rustic wooden door of the study was not Dr Sutton's usual practice. His security system was state of the art, but tonight, he felt the need for extra caution. Living alone meant he had no reason to lock himself in or lock others out of the room. Since his recent appointment as head of the Department of Psychiatry, Sutton had made few friends in the university and had yet to entertain guests in his home. He had muscled in on a position that most of the staff believed should have gone to a local candidate. For this, he did bear some regret, like forgetting insect repellant on a camping trip, and reasoned that the stakes were far higher than this small city with its prestigious, though little, university could appreciate.

His international academic reputation and networks provided a marketing opportunity that the university had been quick to grasp. Sutton's ability to attract international research interest followed by funding was well earned. It was a clear-cut business decision, and loyalties to long-term staff were compromised for the sake of gaining a stronger footing in the international health research industry. The rationale was despised by many academic staff, whom the new managerial elites considered annoyingly antiquated. The former, they believed, luxuriated in cloistered environments, merely feigning commitment to a higher principle of the purpose of education, while in reality they feared change, especially the kind of change that threatened to diminish their overvalued sense of importance in the knowledge community.

In the last few years, morale across the university had fluctuated from bad to toxic. Sutton had inherited an emotional quagmire of defensive and embittered intellectuals who were more than upset by the ongoing restructuring. 'Maybe I should quit and practice psychotherapy,' he quipped as he paced the few feet to the computer station. Sitting somewhat stiffly in the leather chair, with a body still rigidly protesting his rising from a well-deserved slumber, he opened his email.

Subject: Fugue
From: Mathew Ballark
It's happening again, Adrian. I'll be in touch. We found several of them in the same dissociative state, wandering through the city

(post-conference). It's the same diagnosis. Identity loss, certain skills and attributes still in place, no idea who they really are, no recovery yet. Prognosis. Let's hope it's not like the Pacific villages. This has come at a sensitive time. Running the food poisoning story of the Royals affected. Benjamin is on his way. He'll brief you fully.

Ballark's brevity was uncharacteristic. Adrian was accustomed to rather more expressive phraseology from a man who was comfortable with lengthy orations and delighted in the sound of his own voice. Not unlike many of his colleagues, he thought. But brevity meant urgency, and the professor could picture the furrowed brow of his former employer and one-time confidante.

On the surface, Sutton was an orderly man; books, papers, pens all had a special place. There was clinical precision to this orderliness, which was an image he liked to portray and one he too often lived up to. He liked precision, strove for it. It had marked him out early in his undergraduate years, where an A-plus average had earned him a Rhodes Scholarship, and in his post-graduate years, he received an invitation to an elite academic club. He recalled the frothy intellectualism of those days with fondness – the high moral tone and leisurely musings about the fate of the free world, the ethics of biogenetics, the political machinations of globalisation and One World Government.

Adrian had been an intense young man, an idealist with a penchant for perfection, which had afforded a high degree of personal frustration and impatience, particularly with others' perceived mediocrity. The youthful Adrian was somebody others had expected to make a difference, and he had. It had just taken some unexpected turns, the kind of twists that one could not prepare well for. And having a destiny, unlike many of his peers, he thought, consoled the nagging doubt that perhaps, if he hadn't been so arrogant, he could have avoided the creeping isolation he now felt. He carried the emotional distance from his family and those early friendships like an old familiar scarf, readily tossed on the hook in the hallway and worn only on the bleakest occasions.

Since the loss of their unborn child so soon after he and his wife were married and the tragic death of his wife, he had devoted himself to a singular cause – forgetting. Even now, at the age of fifty-two, his blue eyes sparkled at the possible discoveries and advances in his specialist field that might lie ahead. And as long as they were ahead, he felt no reason to dwell in what had been.

Lately, the new demands of holding the chair in this university town half a world away from his Canadian homeland was causing him to settle more for the appearance of order rather than its substance. He thumbed his way through some uncharacteristically loose papers and paper clips searching for a blue-covered manuscript in the drawer. Leaning back, with the document on his lap, he recalled the meeting in Ballark's London office several months back where the title of the spiral-bound manuscript had first caught his attention.

Dissociative Fugue: An Investigation into the Forgotten Malady
Jessica Summer, PhD Draft (final)
Supervisor: Dr Amy Carmichael
Department of Psychiatry
University of Otago

At 3.30 a.m. he turned the final page and mumbled. 'Brilliant. Maybe a little too lateral but well argued. There is an academic future for this young lady,' he judged and ruefully corrected, 'that is if we can get a handle on the causes of the thing before it erases everything'. The temperature was balmy for this time of the morning and sleep inviting. He stretched out on the couch in the study, rubbed his eyes, placed his glasses in their case and sank into the soft, green, leather three-seater. 'Two hours should do it.' He set the alarm for a 5.30 start.

Through the bay window, he could see the city below, humming serenely against the evening sky. The main university library was well lit, although students had left hours ago, and his office, off to the right, lay shrouded by the shadow of the new medical building extension. He allowed himself one final thought, 'Dr Carmichael, life as you know it is about to change.' Outside, a fantail nestled into the slim cover of a kōwhai branch and watched the moon fall.

where the girls are
for KM and DT

Selina Tusitala Marsh

the best men: Part I
for MSP

the rev said
it was PI feminists and fundamentalists
who had problems
with four naked Samoans
at a wedding

where are the women's voices?
why is there so much swearing?

the rev said
the boys said
we're boys
tell the girls
to write their own

the rev said
he got the F-word count
down from 157

to 14
not bad
for a Newton boy

the guests gathered
tickets in hand
lined up TAB stand-like
placing bets on whether
they'd pull it off
backing their favourite actors
dissing the fia shows
nosing ahead for that right seat

academics and
social workers were weary
of watching something so un-pc
but me
I was surprised
laughed
at lampooning
of every
one
every
thing
while Savage and
Nesian Mystik
lifted
me up
beyond the screen
and into a scene of
other brown towns
hue-ing mainstream
viewing
peering down
seeing brown
and white

laughing
complaining
and talking
            talking
                        talking
about what they liked
didn't like
what needed to be done right
and not so white
and not so trite (but that's comedy)

and that was
the real wedding
as kiwi audience
married Polynesian screen.

On Swimming in Vula: Part II

four ladies
three last year
one body of staged water
one body of hair
silhouettes of choreographed meaning
watching and washing
boy stereotypes
away
greasy mechanical constructions
flushed with the kaga mea

fan fish fly high beneath
moana nui
white stick fish whip the air
an ichthys flying

evangelising a freedom in shimmering spray
a lit bit finger
then a school of fingers nibble a lit hand
a kissing siva in a water mirror
like a skimming frigate bird's soaring after its
    own reflection
like the dipped wet curl licking tips of wave
like the hollow cup of hand
beating out a sway
a cocooned watery rhythm
a siva Samoa
a miraculous walking on water
I saw the tsunami in her eyes
the gush would come later
over a $14 cocktail
with something lemony biting my tongue
and three ladies
maybe four next year
talking about where the girls are.

On Smelling Frangipani Perfume:
Part III

noses inclined
they waited for the Velvet Dream curtain to rise
to tama'ita'i skies
and for the dance of perfume vapours
wafting under studio lights
to settle on the bare shoulders
of three bent sisters
wiping the floor
with mops of hair

swirling black in their own galaxy
    of porcelain white
porcelain, of the restroom variety
perfume, of the Janola persuasion
acidic to aching nostrils
armed with Toilet Ducks and pink rubber gloves
the audience see
crushed frangipani petals
pungent and
browning
on porous skin
pungent and
browning of
porcelain
they worship at the
memorial of migrant shift workers
decades of sweepers swooners splashers
a slice of pacific mango
a freshED up production
of a not-so-staged world

mouths and starry eyes
a galaxy of blue collared hopes
a tempest of Caliban's making
a Southern Cross of sisters
pointing to a gravitating
parental centrifugal force
sucking in progeny stars
comet tails
spinning and swirling
like a wet mop in the sky
suds of stars in its wake
as dream bubbles burst
and meteors streak a mile of sisterly connection
affection of the deepest kind
where these celestial bodies

gravitate
in a singular galaxy
they bend and bow from floor to bucket
from good daughterhood to misunderstood
lover to eccentric astronomer
hair parted down her face
a wizened streak to the moon
a thousand black shooting comets from Sina
over her eyes
under her nose
tail spinning through her breath.

Afakasi pours herself afa cuppa coffee

Selina Tusitala Marsh

That was it in a coconut shell. But how to flesh it out? To scrape out the meat? To flake out metaphor, imagery, symbolism and a message? She remembers when the youngest uncle with the dead eyes would sit on the DB crate with an arc of canned metal teeth tied at the end. A delicate skull of coconut palmed and halved by an efficient swipe of the machete. Dig dig scrape dig dig scrape. Afa and her sister would stare at the growing pile of dandruff at his feet. Falling on his cracked toes. Ugly toes. Dead eyes. All the kids stayed away from him.

Afa's thoughts cowered under the shadow of her pen about to trek the unexplored terrain of her paper. Its whiteness mocked her. But hasn't that always been the case? The brown edges of her newly inked words mocked her. Hasn't *that* always been the case? She liked the sound of that first line. She liked its wit, the charm of its rhythm. But nothing would come after that. She was stalled by the intangible voices all vying for attention. Used to being dismissed, they refused to sound above a whisper.

She found herself at the front of a crowded hall, leaning over a tapa-covered podium noosed by happy-coloured lei. She was to give the keynote speech to six hundred freshly capped students. All of Pacific descent. She was here because of her brownness. Specifically, the rarity of her brownness in the upper echelons of the science world. She was the first brown chromosomologist, a specialist in renegade DNA, focusing on the hybrid genome's rejection of the purity of the helix structure. She had discovered it on Lapanaka, a little-known archipelago just a nautical left of Tuvalu and still under the paternal protectorate of New Zealand. She was here to speak as a first, as a brown.

She could feel the ribbon-threaded black betel-nut lei pulsating against her chest. Each nut with its hand-painted blood red mini hibiscus quivering above the tell-tale signs of a treacherous heart. This was not acceptable. She was a professional. Hasn't she made it this far? Hadn't she spoken in front of international audiences in Bordeaux, Kuala Lumpur and San Francisco? Her words were caught in the phlegm of her throat. Did that make them phlegmatic? Still a sense of humour under pressure. Afa marveled at her outward composure and that geeky side of herself that was trying to save her right this minute.

She had prepared an excerpt from a well-known oratorical speech. Honorific and respectful. Geared to gain the aahs and oohs from older brownies flooding the hall. She'd do her mother proud. But then she faltered. Frozen in the deep of their faces, their expectations, her projection of their expectations on how one does brown publicly. Would her second-hand knowledge slap her in the face? Would she lose face? Would they see through her earnest machinations of endeavouring to carry off a seamless cultural performance? She swallowed her borrowed words and cleared her throat. She spoke. In the only tongue she'd ever known. Talofa lava and hello. Welcome honoured guests. Congratulations to the graduating students of ...

This of course, was too awkward to be inked.

Afakasi pours herself afa cuppa coffee
contemplates her full day

Yes. Maybe a poem. Maybe a space-filled, fragmented but titillating poem. No need to be anchored by times, dates, places. Anchors dig. Then wound. Then bleed. Then fester. Nuances. And the creation of. Hinted moments. And suggestions of. Glimpses of colour. And the mixing of on a poetic palette. Less demanding. Less of a mirror held up to one's own face. More complete in its incompleteness. More realised in the va, the spaces in between. Intake of breathe. Pauses of memory. Teasing with tiny gasps of comprehension. An afakasi ambiance.

Afakasi pours herself afa cuppa coffee
contemplates her full day

The media decided it was a front-pager. The first brownie girlie with a rare qualification. 1ZB named her Viva Diva for a day. On graduation day she wore someone else's sky blue pants, bagging at its strung waist. Its unfortunate faded partner, a pillowcase masquerading as a top, completed the tent ensemble. She wandered along shiny hospital corridors in her mother's old kiss-me-don't-miss-me fluffy slippers. She should have been in black. Batman black as her son once described it. A red-and-yellow-trimmed black satin cape. A soft hat sitting smug as a fat black cat on her head. He'd be eight years old, that cat in the hat. But a mother's heroic deeds are mostly done on the side of a rugby field, icing yet another bloody knee. After wiping a bench clean from strategically grated veggies hidden in a shepherd's pie. During the turn of a well-fingered page, cushioned by softly breathing pyjamad bodies. And here. At a hospital bedside of a bone-tumored child and another precautionary CAT scan. She caught the end of her delayed-broadcast interview at the nurse's station and kept the source of her wry smile to herself.

And how her body
Will be read
Every
Which
Way

Every public appearance is a negotiation between earrings. Afa had earrings for Africa. And from Africa too. Stripy zebra ones (so eighties now). Maui shmaui. She's hooked up the whole of Oceania, netted on soft fala hanging on her wall. Coconut shells from Aitutaki. Some wrapped with tapa. Some not. Melted down vinyl triangles from Apia. Some inlaid with pāua. Some not. Pandanus woven stars from Tongatapu. Some dyed. Some not. Woven wired spirals from the $2 Shop. Some pierced with shell. Some not. Polished shell discs from Otara. Some carved. Some not. Ethnicity on a hook. Pick an Oceanic village and be charmed by their sway on the lobe of a lady whose brownness will stump most guesses. Today, she wears simple gold hoops. The mother-of-pearl brooch encircled by green blue cat's eyes will suffice.

but
loose
(so her mother prays)

It's she who lies at the crux of it. Tinā. Like no one else's mother. A face lined with regret and the bitterness of it all. A faife`au's daughter. A black sheep in Samoa. A working teen who would hide her rum in a hollowed-out coconut shell and give it to her father to put in the village's solitary fridge. No one would touch the coconut of the faife`au. Ran away from an Island fool spouting words like alofa and tamaiti. Right into the arms of a mercantile Scotsman. Who was convenient. Who was self-made. Who held a New Zealand passport. Who was twenty-five years her senior. She ran. Right into Bigger Dreams land. They became a KiwiBaconEgg family. As long as mother and children did not compete with the vodka and coke partnership of the father. Which they didn't. He was an absent presence anyway. And she. No church for this reformist. Born again in the house of the un-churched. No falesā, loto, aufaipese, gagana, White Sundays for this one. Except when she lay white tablecloths across the factory floor for the kids' feed at the boozy Christmas parties out at Mangere. She remembers green serviettes on red paper plates smiling back mistletoe and bells, ringing out Happy New Year 1974 in Bigger Dreams land.

(Her mother prays.)

Family meetings were tired orange lounges yawning with brown bodies and coconut oil. Lavalava and bibles and mother being massaged with green and yellow leaves. Fingers of steaming herbs circling towards the ceiling. A gout-ridden man with his swollen purpling foot, skin stretched transparent. An old lady with a lump dangling heavy from the side of her face. Waiting for healing. Kids shushed into bare back rooms. Ripped wallpaper revealing accidental friezes of dancing figures demanding the children guess the nature of their silhouetted souls. In the boredom. Of waiting. Tongues poked and fingers pinched at the otherness of Afa and her sister. Holding pee. The damp stink of the bathroom a deterrent to relief. They escaped outside. Picking up sticks the girls would dig mud pies. Or dare to explore the vacant lot and the beached rusted Triumph with stubborn doors. Bejewelled with webbing in the aftermath of rain. The neighbours had chickens and pigs. They'd hear them through the hedge. Lynn Mall was across the road. And getting bigger. It would swallow up these Victoria Street state houses sooner than anyone expected. The girls went back inside to see if mother was healed yet. Hoping for a slice of bread, pankeke if they were really lucky.

Afakasi pours herself afa cuppa coffee
contemplates her full day
and how her body will be read
every
which
way
but
loose
(so her mother prays).

Real Natives
Talk about Love

Teresia K. Teaiwa

1. On a sea wall

So you don't mind? *No.* You understand? *Yes.* We can still be
friends, you know. *Yeah.* You don't sound convinced. *Whatever.*
Hey … don't be like that. *Like what?* Like this. *Like hurt?* Yeah,
man. I don't want to hurt you. *Well, you have.* Come on. You've
been through worse. *What?* You're a big girl. I know how strong
you are. *What?* You don't need me. I'm not good enough for you.
(She laughs, incredulous.) I've just been a source of amusement for
you. And I enjoyed it, too. But now … *Now, you've found something
more enjoyable.* Someone. *Something.* You know, this bitterness isn't
attractive in you. *Whatever.* Not attractive at all. *You think I give a
shit about what you find attractive now?* Look. Why can't we end this
nicely? *It's already over.* I still do want to be friends, though. *Yeah.*
One day, I'd like you, me and her to all be friends. *Ha!* Really!
You'd like her. *You are really funny, you know that?* I'm glad I can
still make you laugh. *What a laugh.* I'll take you home now. *No.*
It's okay. *I'll walk home.* No, I'll drop you. *No, you'll dump me, you
bastard.* Oh, c'mon. *No. I can walk.* It's not good. I brought you
here. I'll take you back. *I'll take myself back. Thank you very much.*

2. In a coffee shop

I owe you an apology. *Uh-huh.* I'm sorry. *Uh-huh.* This is long overdue. *Yup.* Umm. Look. Part of why I couldn't say this before is ... I knew that anything I said would sound lame. You've heard every excuse under the sun, I bet. *Yup.* Mine's really lame. *Well, let's hear it then.* Okay. Umm. Well. The thing was ... things were going too fast for me. *Uh-huh.* The sexual tension was just too great. *Uh-huh.* I hadn't been with a woman in a really long time. *Uh-huh.* And the pressure just got to me. *Mmm.* You know? *Hmmm.* The pressure to perform was too great. *Hmmm.* I know that doesn't sound like much of an excuse. *Yeah.* I should have been more upfront about it. But I just couldn't face you. So I just stopped calling. *Mmm.* There's no one else. It's just me. *Mmm.* And I just thought that since you had the courage to call me first, then the least I could do was give you an explanation. *Mmm-hmm.* So ... what do you think? *Thanks for the apology.* No hard feelings? *Nah.* Oh, thank you. And you know, if you ever want to go to the movies or get a drink or go dancing, you can call me. *You must be kidding.* You wouldn't call me? *You obviously smoke dope. Look. Take it easy. I'll see you around ... unfortunately. This place is too small.*

3. Outside a nightclub

I'm so sorry. *I don't need another sorry.* I know. But I'm really sorry. *(Her silence)* (His silence) *So where the fuck were you?* I was at my friend's house. I couldn't get a ride. I had no money. He really wanted to get me in trouble with you. So he kept making me drink more grog. *What was the last thing I said to you?* Be on time. *Right. And not only were you not on time. You never even showed up. Until now. Well, you know what? I really worked hard on this show. And this was the last night. So I want to have fun now. But I can't have fun if you're here. So you'd better go.* (His silence) *(Her silence)* I know I fucked up. But is there any way we can fix this? *I don't know.* I'm really sorry. *Yeah. Well, that's just not enough.* I'm so sorry. *Just go.* (His silence) *You need some money to go?* No! *Okay, then. See you later.* (He turns and leaves.)

4. Over the phone

Why won't you come here? I don't want to have to fit into your world. *But you might like it.* I thought we were going to try to meet each other halfway. *Well, that would mean California or something.* Why don't you come back here? *(Her silence)* Things are okay here. I miss you so much. *I miss you, too.* (His silence) *I'm thinking of cutting my hair.* Don't! *It's just getting out of control.* Don't you cut your hair. You'll look like a commie dyke bitch again. *(Her silence)* (His silence) *(Her silence)* I don't know why I love you, but I do. *I love you, too. 'Bye. (She puts the phone down.)*

5. At a party

So, how have you been? *Oh, fine.* Yeah? *Yeah.* I've been wanting to call you. *Yeah?* But … I'm afraid. *Yeah. Don't worry about it.* It's just … too complicated. *Yeah.* It's requiring much more forethought than I imagined. *Yeah. It's alright. You've got more important things to do.* Well, one really important thing. *Yeah. Well, just focus on that. Don't worry about me. Hey, do you want another drink? I'm going to get myself another one.*

6. At another party

Hey, you're really interesting to talk to! *Why, thank you, kind sir!* No, I mean it! Where's your boyfriend? *I don't have a boyfriend.* How come? *What do you mean?* How come you don't have a boyfriend? *I don't need one.* Yeah? *Yeah.*

7. At a restaurant

You won't find what you need here. *What do you mean?* The men here are all idiots. *(She laughs.) You got that right.* You need to go overseas. New Zealand. Or something. *I don't want to go overseas.* Well, then, you'll never find your Mr Right. *Why do you care whether I find him or not?* I care about you. *That's really sweet.* I wish I were younger. *And not married.* (He smiles.) *Look. I'm not looking. So don't worry about it.* You deserve to be happy. *I am happy.* (His silence) *I enjoy our lunches.* I enjoy them, too. Why don't we have drinks after work sometime? *Nah. Lunches are good. Drinks are not good. For me, anyway.* Okay. We'll stick to lunches. *Thank you.* No, thank you. I could sit and listen to you for hours. I don't know what it is … I think it's your eyes. *Hmmm.* Thank you, my dear. Can I give you a lift home? *Thanks. I'll be alright. Gotta run some errands in town. Thanks. We'll be in touch, eh? Bye.*

8. In another coffee shop

I've always wanted to be a writer. *(She nods.)* There are so many things I want to write about. But I guess I'd start with my grandmother. I want to write her life. I want to document the experience of her generation. What it was like for her to be married to my grandfather. To have all her children. And grandchildren. *(She suppresses a yawn.) Why don't you write about yourself?* No, no. I think it would be much more interesting to write about my grandmother. *Well, start writing.* Yes. I'd like it to be a novel. A sort of fictional memoir. *Uh-huh.* Yes. I think I shall start my novel. I've had this idea for a long time. *Mmm.* I've always wanted to be a writer. But my father wanted me to be a doctor. Or a lawyer. You know. The colonial dream. *Yeah.* And when I chose not to study medicine or law, my father stopped talking to me. *Wow. (She is bored.)* Yes. For a whole year, he wouldn't talk to me. *Wow.*

9. At home

I know what you're looking for. *What do you think I'm looking for?*
Companionship. I know. *So?* So … you know, if you hadn't broken
so many hearts in the past, you wouldn't be in this situation. *I never
broke any men's hearts.* You hurt their feelings. *Okay, maybe I hurt
some guys' feelings.* And feelings are close to the heart. *Okay, okay.*
This is what you get for being like that. *So you're saying I deserve
this?* No. I'm just saying … that word gets around. People here
know how you've treated men in the past. *You know … I don't know
what you're talking about. I am no heartbreaker.* That's for sure. *It's my
heart that's getting broken all over the place.* Now. But before, it was
you just loving and leaving them. *Please!* You're the kind of woman
… when young guys come to ask me for advice, I say, look at my
eldest daughter. Stay away from women like her. *Gee, thanks, Dad.
You're a real sport.*

10. At yet another party

I'm still wearing your ring. Wow. *Do you want it back?* No. It's yours.
No, take it. No, please keep it. It's yours. *It's the only ring a man's
ever given me.* It's yours. *I don't think I'll ever get married.* You will.
Look at me. *(She laughs cynically.)* Look, you'll find the right person
for you. *Yeah.* It's nice being like this with you. *Yeah. How come we
always get along so well?* (He smiles.) *(She sighs.)* I'll take you home.
Okay.

11. On a verandah

I hope I'm not boasting, but I must say that I am a qualified linesman.
Really? Yup. I am a qualified linesman. *What does that mean?* I am
qualified as a linesman. *Uh-huh. So why aren't you working as a*

linesman? Oh, cos this arsehole at work got me into trouble with the foreman. *Oh.* But I'm also an experienced butcher. *Really?* Yup. I really know my meat. You can ask me anything about meat. I know it. Next time you want to buy some meat let me know. I can tell you what's the best. *Oh, okay.*

12. Over a candlelight dinner

I remember the first time I met you. *Yeah?* I thought you were American. *Really?* And I thought you had nice feet. *What? (She laughs.)* Yeah. (He laughs.)

Smiles and Transactions

Angela Gribben

She scanned the terminal below to see if her husband had come to pick her up. Making her way down the stairs, she was disappointed to see her name on a black plastic board, which read CORPORATE CABS – MRS RYAN in white letters, evenly spaced and placed with care by the taxi driver holding it. She ignored him and walked towards the luggage-claim area.

Mrs Ryan was accustomed to this part of the domestic airport. She made a habit of taking her mark on a piece of silvery gum stamped into the carpet closest to the black rubber screen that separated her from the luggage workers. Hearing thuds and thumps behind the black screen, she imagined possessions being thrown upon the conveyer belt, regardless of whether they were marked with large red FRAGILE stickers or not. Ordinarily, Mrs Ryan would have made a game out of guessing which type of luggage would be first to make it through the black screen, but this time she watched her taxi driver.

The first thing she noticed about him was that he was old, maybe in his late sixties. The other was his hair. Glistening white and polished from years of combing, it was neatly packed, much like it would have been as a young man, combed slightly upwards from the top of the forehead then levelled around the crown. He stood motionless, with the slightest smile, holding the name board as though waiting for his photograph to be taken, waiting for a Mrs Ryan to appear. Irritated by his dutifulness, Mrs Ryan was late to attend to her small black suitcase moving past. She pushed past a young Japanese couple, lifted her bag and made her way to her driver.

'Mrs Ryan?'

'Yes.'

'I thought I had the wrong arrival time.' He was surprised she had already retrieved her bag. 'May I take that for you?'

'Yes, here.' Mrs Ryan answered abruptly, noticing he had an accent. It was both crisp and heavy on the ears at the same time. She tried to match the accent and colour of his skin. Light skin. Australian? No. White skin. American? No definitely not. Pink skin. From Europe somewhere?

'My car is just outside here.' He was a clean-shaven man, with elongated features as though his ears, forehead, cheeks and nose had failed to stop growing through the years. His cheeks fell slightly over the collar of his white shirt, supported further by a stiff crimson tie. Wearing a black wool suit, he had a gold name tag attached to the lapel, and it read 'Mr Forrester'.

Mr Forrester started the ignition and simultaneously pressed the taximeter.

'Where're we heading?'

'Herne Bay.'

There were three long lanes of taxis to her right, beyond a single row of concrete barriers. They were all white sedans with the odd white van here and there. Their owners were all male, with various tones of dark skin, all hoping for fifty-dollar-or-more passengers. She could recognise some physical differences between the drivers — some had turbans, others shaved heads, many had eyes shaped like commas that had fallen on their backs — but these differences were not enough for her to establish with confidence where they were from. Still she guessed, hoping it would make her feel better about herself, that she knew something they did not.

Mrs Ryan was thirty-six years old. Her golden-syruped complexion, full lips and large dark eyes gave her a beauty that would have coerced much attention from men, but her short black hair and shadow of fine hairs around her hairline and upper lip, gave her an androgynous appearance that made her and other women feel comfortable. A petite woman, she wore a crisp blue suit and matching low-heeled shoes. As a senior sales representative for a large cosmetics company, she had learnt to tolerate wearing make-up, wearing the minimum amount possible while preserving the image of the company.

Outside her window, she watched as they passed a school park. It was late afternoon, yet the sun was still bright. They were driving in the shadows of tall trees lining the borders of the park. The sun flashed colourless light through the spaces of the trees in fast intervals, like a strobe light, irritating her.

'Where are you from?' Mr Forrester asked.

She scowled at him. 'Excuse me?'

'Where are you from? You look like you don't come from this country.' Mr Forrester continued, unaware of Mrs Ryan's glare.

Mrs Ryan thought of the taxi drivers she saw at the taxi rank. Her curiosity about their origins was intoxicating. It made her feel unfamiliar – like a tourist. She answered Mr Forrester, not for his sake, but for her own. 'I was born here.'

'Surely, your parents are not from here?' He looked disappointed, like he had tried to guess where she was from and failed. 'Where are they from?'

'They are Samoan.'

'Samoan? Do your people have independence?'

She thought it was an odd question. What did it matter to him whether Samoa was an independent country or not? Besides, she didn't care about history. She shrugged, hoping to deflect his interest in the topic. It worked.

'I'm from Zimbabwe,' he said.

So the accent is African, she thought to herself.

'I have been here four years now, and you know something? I still can't get used to paying for food here. I grew everything myself over there. Yes, I did. I owned a dairy farm, but I grew fruit and vegetables too. The best potatoes I ever had were mine. Straight out of the ground and into a pot of boiling water – the only way to cook them.' He paused. 'And the land – so many beautiful animals you can't get anywhere else in the world, plants you can't get anywhere else in the world. So green, so lush, so beautiful. And the soil, the colour, it always looked like it was on fire.'

Raving old man she thought. Why the hell did he come here then if it was so beautiful? She wished some other taxi driver had picked her up.

As though he sensed her contempt he explained. 'I fled the country, you know. The blacks took my land, my farm, everything.'

Mrs Ryan felt uneasy about the word 'blacks'. She wondered what he thought of her dark skin. Was she a 'black' too or did he have another name for her?

'One morning, I got a phone call from a neighbour warning they were breaking into farms close by. I didn't want to believe it. Then I could hear shouting and screaming from as far as two kilometres away. Awful, I tell you. I got out just minutes before they got to my farm – an armed gang of them on a truck. They wrecked my home, taking what they wanted, beating my workers and smashing their homes. They burnt everything. Everything. There was nothing left.'

For the next few kilometres she listened to him. About how he came to New Zealand. About his daughter, Julia, who had fallen in love with a New Zealander and moved here almost ten years ago. Julia was his only child. Thirty-seven years old and no children. He was one of the lucky ones with somewhere to go. Thank God for his daughter, he said.

And his wife died seven years ago from cancer. Awful disease. It took her for no good reason at all; she didn't smoke or drink. It made no sense. He would not wish cancer on his worst enemies. Not that he had any. He was, in a strange way, glad his wife did not live through the loss of their farm. It would have broken her, he said. An amazing woman, always concerned for other people and their well-being. Even their workers were well looked after. His wife always made sure their workers' children were well stocked for school with pencils, books, whatever they needed. He smiled. She was an amazing baker, made the best lemon pie he ever tasted.

She took his heart with her when she died. There was a black hole in his chest. No one could get to him, and he could get to no one. Mrs Ryan felt depressed, and she felt more depressed when he told her he was not close to his daughter.

'She lives her life, and I live mine,' he said.

Mrs Ryan felt sorry for him, and wanted to steer the conversation away from Mr Forrester and his terrible stories but didn't know what to say.

'And you? Any children?' he asked.

Relieved for the change in subject, she felt like she was more in the mood to talk. 'No, none.'

'Too busy with work?'

'Yes and no. I can't stand them.'

He laughed. 'You sound like my daughter. And what do your parents think?'

'About me not having children? They are not happy at all.'

'No brothers or sisters?'

'I've got a younger brother.'

'Maybe your parents can have grandchildren from him?'

'No.' She laughed.

'Oh?'

'He's gay.' She caught herself. Perhaps she should have censored this from Mr Forrester, however, she was surprised to hear him laugh.

'Tell your parents to get used to the idea of getting to know you both more!'

Mrs Ryan relaxed a little more.

'And your husband does not want children?

'No. He's not too keen on them either.'

'That's all that matters then, isn't it? You both want the same things. That's good. If it was anything else, you two would have problems.' He paused to look both ways at a large intersection. 'How long you been married for?'

'Seven years.'

'That's wonderful. What does he do?'

She didn't want to talk about her husband or her marriage. Mrs Ryan moved the conversation away. 'Have you many friends in New Zealand?'

'Two,' he reported. 'They're taxi drivers. Indians. We meet for lunch on Sundays; they cook their food, and I cook mine. They're vegetarians. Then we sit and watch the sports channel. I have Sky you see, so whatever is on, we watch it. We don't say much, we just sit and watch. How about you Mrs Ryan? Do you have friends?'

'Yes.' She lied. She had four close friends from university, but as they started having children, Mrs Ryan quickly grew bored of their conversations about lack of sleep, nappy brands, teething, breastfeeding and remedies for cracked nipples. She started declining invitations for first- and second-year-old birthday parties. Eventually the invitations no longer arrived in the post, and the phone calls stopped. 'We do the same thing – we get together on Sundays for lunch, too.'

There was silence for a moment before Mrs Ryan reached for her diary in her bag, writing her name and number on an empty page. She imagined herself in his kitchen on a Sunday, sharing her problems with Mr Forrester while preparing chop suey and taro. She would show him how to cut the skin away from the taro, revealing its flesh, speckled with brown spots like blackheads on pink skin. She looked at her number, checking it was legible, printing over it again, thinking of a way she could hand it to him. Thinking of something delicate and light to say. Imagining him calling her for some company.

It was almost six thirty when the taxi turned into her street. Mrs Ryan wished she had told Mr Forrester to take the longer route, along Mt Eden Road, down Newton Gully then along Ponsonby Road, through all the traffic lights. 'Stop right here, thanks.'

Mrs Ryan's house, a large beige villa, newly renovated with its tropical-themed garden, suddenly looked immodest to her. Her husband's car was not in the driveway, nor was it parked on the street. Mr Forrester pulled on the handbrake. He turned to her and smiled.

Without warning she blurted out, 'My husband does want to have children.'

There was silence for a moment. She thought he had not heard her.

'My husband wants children—'

'Yes.' He reached for his receipt book inside the glove box. 'That will be seventy-three dollars and thirty-five cents, thank you.'

She was taken aback. Ordinarily she would have cash ready to give before the taxi fare was announced. 'Oh.' She opened her handbag to look for her wallet and laughed nervously. 'So you see we really do have problems.'

'Yes, Mrs Ryan.' He seemed unruffled by her confession, writing on the receipt book.

'My name is Ana.' It irked her a little every time he called her 'Mrs Ryan'. It made her feel old. Pulling out four twenty-dollar notes, she pulled on the corners to be sure they were uncreased.

'Mrs Ryan—'

'Did you not hear what I said?'

'Yes, your name is Ana.' He tore the receipt away from the book.

'No, what I was saying about my husband.'

'Yes.' He held out the receipt to her. 'Here we are.'

'Mr Forrester, did you hear what I said?'

'Here.'

'Oh, I get it.' Mrs Ryan realised he was brushing her off.

'Take it.' He persisted, making a slight movement to move the receipt closer to her. 'Mrs Ryan—'

'No, I understand!' she interrupted, shoving her wallet and diary back into her bag and opening the door. 'Open the boot!'

'Do you lie to your husband too?' he said calmly.

She snatched the receipt and threw the money at him. This startled him. He quickly threw his elbow up to protect himself, then, realising it was money, he moved his right hand swiftly to trap the notes against his left arm.

There was silence for a moment.

'Open the goddamn boot!'

'It's okay, Mrs Ryan. I understand.'

Mrs Ryan watched him as he counted the money. She waited for him for a moment, expecting him to say something more. He turned to her and without looking at her, he handed her some coins, pulled on a tab beneath his seat, then opened his door and walked to the back of the taxi. Mrs Ryan stepped out onto the footpath.

'Here's your bag.' He placed her bag on the ground in front of her.

She was about to say something, but as she observed Mr Forrester, a knowledge of something familiar lingered in his eyes, and she stopped. It wounded her. She realised at that moment they shared a loneliness suppressed by smiles and transactions. She quickly retreated and held her stare until she was a few steps away.

'Have a good evening, Ma'am.'

She forced an expression of gratitude and turned away from him. She walked up the stairs of her front porch and listened to Mr Forrester as he shut the door of his taxi and drove away. She thought of her name and number she had written for Mr Forrester, it remained untorn from her diary. It occurred to her that she did not ask him for his first name.

An educated perspective

Karlo Mila

After I say I am 'Tongan'
the Tongan PhD
says that she can tell the difference
between
real Tongans
and those who are not.
Real Tongans say
'Donga'
Like, Doe a Deer a female deer.
Those who are not real Tongans
say 'Tonga'
like, Tea, a drink with jam and bread.
They have
Fa
a
long long way to go.

Four Poems and Sione's Wedding

Karlo Mila

The Best Boys
Yeah, 'Get the girls to write their own.'
But with all due respect to Oscar,
it's just not gonna be a comedy,
if you know what I'm saying.

Yeah, those boys know freedom
like flying foxes in the night
old-school styles / two-door waka
sailing streets / fishing with new nets
you know the drill …
Bat wings
dipping into K-Rd
caves
winging their way
across the divide
scoring a rugby blonde
and back again
for another try

lady luck lucking
mouths fire trucking

drive thru drives
double-double standards
burgers with fries

and milk shakes shaking all around
'damn right, it's better than yours'

Followed religiously
by wooden pew penance
and prayer promises.

In the mix of all of that,
It's just not so fun
having to be the princess.

Riddle me ree
can you tell me?
'How does a wet
dream island girl get
to wear white
at Sione's wedding?'

Where are the girls?
Same old roly-poly roles
dusky maiden in her little lavalava
fertilising the taro patch
and the mum in her mumu
modern-day Mary, her afro like a halo
hands clasped in prayer
for the sins of her sons.

Hmm, it seems we're either hula
or hipping it
either on your arm or
talking to your hand
same old hibiscus
behind the ear.

I mean, come on,
it's called BRO-town mate.

The sisters are still in between lives
that haven't been written yet.

Where the girls are
You'll find us in
the narrow lines
of poetry
where heliaki*, hue
and alliterated affection
blurs all that sex
and sweat and shame
into art.

Water lily maidens
emitting frangipani perfume
like in some soft Monet
moaning gently like rain
pastel and palatable
to our aunties
who'd turn in their graves
like weeds
if we told the seedy truth.

It is all framed
ever so respectfully
lei-ed on a wall

never
laid

bare.

*Tongan = metaphor

Our Stories Are within Us

Cherie Barford

Our stories are within us. You'll find them encoded in genealogies, embedded in our hearts, imprinted in our minds. They migrate with the tongues that tell them, flourish in the presence of orators and gossips and are readily transported to the arenas of lotu and aiga, where they open and close wallets, elevate and deprave souls, win and lose wars.

Some stories cling to the outside world once they're told. They seep into shadows, harbour with bitterness and grief, churn fists into flesh in the pissy corners of derelict streets. Others laugh from the necks of bottles or froth from aluminum cans onto pandanus mats in suburban lounges. Then, there are the stories that crystallise into swinging hips and hula hands or bounce off hats and rafters in churches where not-so-innocent tongues sing glory hallelujah.

Stories are everywhere. They lurk in unlikely places, forming and growing like children, connecting us to a myriad of worlds. They make us laugh. They make us cry. They make us human.

Stories can be forgotten or die out. Local stories can be ousted by the stories of strangers living in faraway lands. Satellites beam these people onto screens that light up our homes. Neighbourhoods relinquish their communal memories for the roller-coaster lives of screen characters they emulate but will never meet.

But truly precious stories, those that hold sacred truths within them, can never be lost. They are kept intact by the universe itself. They exist beyond everything we can touch and name. They are in our blood, and like red hibiscus burnt by frost, recover and reveal themselves again. These stories are so powerful that only the pure of heart can carry them between worlds and survive. They change lives, and their coming is signaled by the stars.

Such a story arrived recently in a small coastal village in the Pacific. A child awoke one night, overcome by fever and vivid dreams. Her delirium shred the mosquito net and woke the entire village.

The quietest elder in the village, one so quiet some thought him mute, entered the thatched hut and elbowed the girl's parents aside. She'd collapsed and lay still as if already dead. The elder knew he was born for this night. He started chanting in a voice that carried through the heavens. He chanted throughout the night – guiding the girl's soul back to her sleeping mat and anchoring it to her body as the stars gave way to dawn.

When the sun rose, the child sat up and recited lost chains of ancient genealogies that linked the people to the gods and the village lands. When she finished, she collapsed into a deep sleep, but the elder, his purpose done, lay down and died.

The villagers wailed and gripped each other. They looked to their priest and chief for guidance, but they were holding the elder and weeping. Then something happened as the story coursed through their veins, travelled to their toes, the tips of their waxy ears and the hollow spaces behind their eyes.

The people began to wriggle and cough as darts of recognition pierced their hearts and opened their minds. The genealogies triggered memories they didn't know they had. Rocks, trees and marks on the land seemed as familiar as the smiles of loved ones. They remembered who they were and where they came from. They understood that the sea, the land and the sky were within them and without at the same time. The village woke up.

The very next day they said 'no' to the land developer from the transnational company who'd promised them electricity and every appliance under the sun.

The next week they said 'no' to politicians who'd promised them jobs in the high-rise hotel planned for the land beside the river that gushed into the sea.

The next month they said 'no' to policemen who tried to evict them from the foreshore and tore up the memorandum of understanding their chief had declined to sign with the Minister of Economic Development.

Their boats, fishing nets and pick-up trucks were confiscated. Their plantations were trampled by herds of cattle that appeared out of nowhere. Their houses mysteriously burnt to the ground, and all the pigs and chickens were poisoned.

They were labelled 'terrorists', and the army planted barbed wire instead of trees in a ring around the village. No one was allowed to trade with them, give them food or medicine or publish their story. They were outcasts on their own island.

But the story fed them, kept them strong. The people smashed their battery radios and burnt the pamphlets planes dropped on them from above. They reconnected with legends, healed their hearts, replaced knowledge with wisdom and stepped in and out of courtrooms and prison cells with grace and fortitude.

The truth refused to be hidden. It leaked out and was aired around the world. The villagers' story was beamed into the living rooms of strangers in faraway places, inspiring both the dispossessed and couch potatoes to rise up and get a life.

The villagers are still living their collective story and fighting to keep the land intact. They have rewritten history books and redrawn maps. They have renamed places and each other. And all the while, they listen to the inner voice that links them to the stars.

'It's like this,' their chief said. 'Everyone has stories. They come from what we call daily life and from the worlds between worlds that we dream and fly in. There's a tusitala in all of us, just waiting to get out. That's where they are. Our stories are within us.'

Connections

Cherie Barford

on sunday the priest said *teu le va*
make presentable the distance
between you and the other

there's no such thing as empty space
just distances between things

made meaningful by fine lines
connecting designs and beings
in the seen and unseen worlds

distances can be shortened
made intimate or dangerous

or lengthened
until the connection weakens
finally withers away

★★★★★★

on monday the chief evicted
the diving school from the island

said sailboats and men in black suits
upset ancestors visiting the bay

the instructor packed his gear
waved goodbye with two fingers

the chief smiled
lit a match

★★★★★★

on tuesday I swam with a green turtle
and an old man riding an iron bike
stopped to greet me

we shook hands

not a city-corporate shake
just a gentle slipping
of fingertips over palms

like origami cranes
delicately pressing
their bills together

a hongi of sorts

★★★★★★

on wednesday we drove inland
past columns of limestone
where birds huddle in nooks
overgrown by banyan roots

banyans start as flimsy seeds
dropped from heaven
onto unsuspecting hosts

their roots twirl down
strangling flourishing trees
as they grope for the ground

we stopped at one banyan
more majestic than others

a grizzly man in track pants
materialised at our side

can we take photos?

he smiled slowly

told us he was the guardian
of the cyclone stone
hidden at the base of the tree

hands on hips
he posed for the camera

we took three pictures

none of them turned out

★★★★★★

on thursday children playing hide 'n' seek
dashed out of their hidey holes
to watch me walk by

I'm the only blue-eyed woman
with frizzy hair on this island

they lifted sunglasses off my nose
peered at me up close

then ran away to spy safely
as I fended off the hungry village dogs

it was a test of sorts

they emerged when the last mongrel
had yelped and slunk away

they'd no idea
I could kick and throw stones
before I could walk

★★★★★★

on friday time melted
on a beach interrupting cliffs

where feral donkeys meander
past magical caverns
sharks enter with moonbeams

and leave as beautiful people
with decorative trailing braids

on the ridge of this world
a warrior ran with his club
towards the towering cliffs
and the chasm that breaks them

the enemy closed in
their breath humming
like coconut-leaf whizzers

their feet pounding louder
than bamboo stamping tubes

he jumped the impossible breach
invocations and ancestors buoyed him up
bridged him to the other side

while beneath the cliffs
waves slapped rocks
senseless

★★★★★★

today is saturday

I've bought a new siapo
for the overcrowded living room

it's harmonious

the land, sea and sky are in accord
the motifs complement each other
everything's connected

which reminds me

I'm still trying to measure
the distance of our connection

have even thought of painting
my body onto yours

it'll fit

we could do it in the backyard
under the banana trees

where roosters flap their wings
and puff out their chests
for the squawking hens

who scratch in the dirt with chicks
they peck to keep in order

huh?

★★★★★★

Pacific Migration

Daren Kamali

This poem is dedicated to the movement,
the movement of our Pacific people.

An Island boy grows up in paradise,
surrounded by the ocean, mountains, rivers,
and serene blue skies.
Growing up in the village of Veisari,
On the island of Viti Levu.
He remembers gathering firewood in the forest
he remembers villagers chanting a Fijian chorus.
'Sa kau cake mai oqo'*
'Someday our Pacific people will rise'
The day comes for the boy to travel overseas.
He grows into a man in a foreign land.
This is Pacific migration.
A movement from Island days and nights
to Big City life.
He now lives life on the City Streets,
he's home away from home.
Today to remember it all
he gazes at an Island map stuck to his wall.
Gone are the days of swimming and fishing with the
villagers.
Gone are the days of innocent fun under the tropical
sun.
In his heart remains his Island home,

The Island man takes his home wherever he goes.
On his journey he chants this Fijian song,
'Sa kau cake mai oqo …'

* A Fijian hymn

The Return (Extract)

Priscilla Rasmussen

I stand on Wellington's Petone foreshore and wonder what all the fuss is about. But then, I've been doing that for years.

My Uncle Will, he just loves this beach. And he is always eager to get to the sea. I cringe and I smile and try not to let my New Zealand family see what I see – that this is no beach at all.

Today of all days, in the middle of spring, people are walking along barefoot. Some are even dipping in their toes and feeling the promise of some odd season that disguises itself as a Wellington summer. During actual summer, the sun rises to the highest and pierces you with its rays. And just when you relax in its warmth, it hides behind a cloud and teases you until you start to shiver. Yes, I believe the seasons in Wellington are up to some trickery!

Petone foreshore looks more like a set in those western movies my uncle likes. It has rows of flaxen bushes, which act like desert doors, and a long, thin, dark, sandy shore strewn with dead logs and twigs and shells and stones of all sizes. Then there's the harbour. It changes colour with the weather. Today, I see it as a greyish kind of green, if you believe that to be a colour. You would think a sea would be blue. But the seas I have seen have been the cleanest of blue, so that anything else is a totally different colour.

There is an island smack bang in the middle of this description by the name of Somes Island. Uncle Will tells me Samoans were imprisoned there many years ago during the war. Samoans on Somes! He said they were Samoans who were German, and they couldn't speak English. This is very easy for me to understand.

What is difficult to believe is that there is any other Samoan who has looked harder or longer at this cold green harbour than me.

Today, my Uncle Will and Auntie Lei and their children have come to Petone foreshore to celebrate my birthday. I am happy for them to host a party for my twenty-one years of age. I've been living in Wellington all of eleven years. And considering I was ten when I left Samoa, I've been in New Zealand more years than I've been out. But I don't feel the last eleven years – not the way I felt the first ten. But here I am – sitting on a Samoan mat on a blustery beach – pretending, like I know my auntie is, that I've never experienced a more beautiful isle-like setting than this.

The sea that laps the Wellington coastline is the first real memory I have of coming to New Zealand eleven years ago. It looked fierce and unfriendly. The second memory I have is a not much better. I had arrived at the airport less than two days after being taken from my home, and my strange new caramel-coloured family took me directly to Oriental Parade for an ice cream. My mother's sister's husband – a pale man with hair like fire and an equally warm heart – thought it would be a treat. I'd never had an ice cream before.

The deliciousness of the ice cream didn't last too long. I was frightened into a mid-air lick when my younger cousins, four and eight, started yelling and pounding their feet in the store. I looked frantically around the shop at people who seemed to take no notice. And then to my bewilderment, the chaos stopped when two glass bottles of black soda were shoved in their outstretched hands. That was the first introduction I had into the ways in which my new life differed from the old. I was so taken aback I hadn't noticed the sweet white stickiness running all down my arms and into my jumper. It was at that instant I thought of my own younger sister – the horror of our parting moments – and my heart grew still.

It was just as well we stepped out onto the pavement and into Wellington's wind – oh, how it's been so kind! It soon rid me of the anguish of thinking about my family I left behind. And no sooner had I licked all the sweetness off my arm, my nicely combed hair blew up and around and back down into the Tip Top cone. I ate it anyway, to my cousins' disgust, hair and all – the coldness shaking me inside. That night, I couldn't bear to tell them how chilly I felt, inside and out, and spent the next week sick in bed because of it.

But here we are, back at the beach over ten years later but on the opposite side of the harbour. The memories of that day as clear as our spring sky – the sea looking as uninviting as ever and circling seagulls that I fear will land on my head and leak all my secrets that they simply must know because they are scavengers with no shame.

My younger cousins are playing out on the sand now, so I join them with their twisted dead-wood sticks. We have fun marking the dirt-coloured sand with letters and pictures of smiling faces. I'm using my stick to draw the amount of money I make a week at the mail centre. The numbers shine like stars in my head. I am so proud. When I give my auntie my weekly pay cheque, she is just as proud. And I dream of the things I could do back home with all that money. And I imagine the look on my family's faces. One day, with money in my wallet, gifts in my suitcase and forgiveness in my heart, I will return.

My drawings in the sand have taken me halfway down the beach. And for now, the sea foam has settled in my markings, pulling them into the sea and taking my numbers with them. And as I look across to the island of Somes, I know I am not the first person to be plucked from the shade of a pua tree to be stored on a distant shore. And I take comfort in this solemn sea that is the Wellington harbour. For my story will be told. And it is this benevolent ocean that will take me home on the breast of a warmer wave.

★★★★★★

Herr Wolf passed the ball for the very last time. So the game ended, and there was much fuss on the makeshift football pitch, which took up most of the exercise yard, in the small encampment on the tiny internment island.

Dr Meyer was livid. As the only German medical officer in the camp, he was stern in his warning to Gottfried Wolf, secretary to the former Chief Justice Herr Tecklenberg, about his ill health. The old man's lungs were poorly and not coping on this chilly island in the middle of Wellington harbour.

He had reminded Gottfried the reason he had been transferred to the German colony of Samoa in 1909 was because at the end of his bureaucratic career an empathetic boss was concerned about his aversion to the cold. The weather was crippling at the best of times in Berlin and Gottfried was not coping. His employer had been right. Samoa was warmer and lengthened the clerk's life by years. Now, on this tiny, wet island exposed to cruel southerlies, he was pronounced dead.

Herr Baer and Herr Lottlamp were beside themselves. They hadn't exactly invited Gottfried, all of seventy, to join their game of football, knowing Dr Meyer held grave concerns with his growing cough. Then they really hadn't intended to let him get wind of the ball. But nothing could stop the old man from making his mark on the small makeshift field that day. He was excited. He had heard rumblings in the New Zealand ranks that the Germans in the camp who were married to Samoan natives were more than likely be able to return to their adopted home. Technically, their families in the New Zealand territory of Western Samoa were now under the protection of the British Empire.

Some laughed amongst themselves, not cruelly, that the twin boys Gottfried had produced with a local Samoan woman had put life back into the old man's veins. Some mumbled that it was cruel of the authorities to play with their minds, knowing how much some missed their agreeable Samoan women and free-spirited half-caste children.

Dr Meyer shook his head in disappointment as he leaned into the old man's body, wiping the fresh foam from Gottfried's mouth with his thick woollen gloves and gently closing his eyelids. The small German contingent, which consisted of the doctor, the former Chief Justice of Samoa, a magistrate, agricultural officer, a surveyor and a diplomatic clerk, soon gathered around, crossed themselves and said The Lord's Prayer. Andre Lottlamp cried.

Shortly after the seizure of German-ruled Samoa in 1914 by New Zealand, under the British Empire, the handful of government workers had been shipped to an internment camp on Somes Island in New Zealand's capital. That capture, as Andre recalled, was four months after a ceremony at the Catholic Church at Matafele, where Gottfried's twin boys were baptised Gottfried and Karl Wolf. Andre was the godfather, and he had made a promise in front of the father, the Father, the Son and Holy Ghost to nurture these tiny boys. Now, their father was dead. Andre said five Hail Marys.

Herr Tecklenberg, still respected as the former deputy leader of an important colony, demanded that the shocked New Zealand guards on duty provide a priest. It wasn't an unusual request from the Germans, but the nature of the request was. The internment camp for enemy aliens had only seen one death when in 1914 Herr Landgraf had keeled over after carrying water up the wharf.

After that, the island authorities had become more vigilant, and five Germans with signs of illness had been transferred to a hospital where they later died. A man, known as Hugo, died of exhaustion early in the morning of 31 July 1918 on the Petone foreshore during a four-man escape attempt. The guards had not seen any of this first-hand; it had not been while under their watch. They liked Gottfried, he was a harmless happy old man, who was often assigned to aid in their duties. So they had delighted in telling him what they had recently heard.

And it was this slip of information that had inflamed the old man's heart with a new surge of hope. Herr Gottfried Wolf wanted desperately to go home. To his whitewashed cottage in the shade of beloved banyans – to his railway station of a household where his sons would weave in and out of the arms of female family members. To his place on the hill.

And as the camp on the tiny internment island in the middle of the Wellington harbour turned in a flurry of post-mortem human activity, a single soul rose from a body.

It turned to look down at the wiry corpse with shocking white hair and faded tan. As it moved skyward, it passed its eye over the sorrow-filled compatriots and sympathetic onlookers. It took in the outline of the encampment, the shape of the island and the breadth of its shores. And then it stopped.

The island held him captive. He knew that long after his body was buried, the soldiers and prisoners had left the island and the war was won and lost, he would remain. But his determination, as in life, was adamant. He would return home. So he would wait. And he would tell his story many times to the sea, and it would listen.

So, when a wave eventually washed upon his tiny island that whispered a tale of longing for the home he missed, he listened. And the ghost of Gottfried rejoiced. For the tale was not an isolated one. One by one, they came in their hundreds, until a tale of love and betrayal kept returning on the tide, pulling at the old ghost, lost in the ebb and flow. And after years of waiting and hoping, the ghost of Gottfried knew that this was the tale to take him home. And so, he waited where the seeking would find him.

A Mother's Love

Noelle Nive Moa

She walks right past me.

The smell of the streets lingers in her hair as she tries unsuccessfully to smooth it behind her ears. A mass of wild curls that have seen gentler days when loving hands would comb the sweet scent of fagu'u Samoa through that black, brilliantined hair.

Falling to her hips and swaying in seductive rhythm as she walked through the village, the villagers knew that she would marry a rich palagi and move to Niu Sila and live in a two-storey house with a swimming pool and drive a big fancy car. A black car. As black as that beguiling mane that whispered secrets like the darkest night.

She sits down on the wood-splintered bench in front of McDonalds, covering a runaway's signature with trousers that had been donated to the Mission by someone who realised they would never wear them again – at least not in this century. A pair of giggling girls sit down next to her but then hastily retreat as they anticipate a familiar request that is to be uttered from the cracked dry lips of the bedraggled looking woman whom they've seen frequent Queen Street from time to time. She throws back her head and laughs. Her yellowing teeth seem to quiver in her parched mouth as a throaty whisky rasp issues forth from her lungs, leaving a foam of saliva around the corners of her lips.

The harsh wilderness of urban dwellings, and years spent trying to conquer that wilderness, has left her lost and as feral as the stray cats that used to wander around her council flat scavenging for food. *People are funny, so funny,* she thinks. It's much easier to laugh at others than face the cold, stinging hurt that sits in the pit of your stomach, interrupted at times by long, loud growls.

She married a palagi. An obvious choice befitting an afakasi teine from Aleisa. But he wasn't just a palagi, he was an American. He worked at Splendor, having transferred from San Diego to become its Pacific agent in Apia. His company specialised in Polynesian oils, having realised the potential earnings for the exotic oils in the lucrative market of cosmetics. A market forever hungry for new products that claimed to eradicate unsightly lines and prolong the youthful appearance you had at twenty, even though you're now forty-five, with three kids, a mortgage and bills coming out of your ass.

He was thirty-six, and she was nineteen. But that didn't matter because he had the sun-tanned appearance of a Californian golden boy. His athletic prowess on the tennis courts kept him as active and agile as any twenty-six-year-old. But his charisma and confidence could only have been acquired through the maturity of his years. He charmed her, just as he was charmed in return. The lo'omatua cried their approvals, the men stood with squared shoulders, and the young girls sighed with envy and wistfulness.

She gave him a daughter at twenty-one. Her hair was the colour of sand at Lefaga Beach and her eyes were as blue as day as her mother's hair was as black as night.

She pulls out a dirty plastic bag from her pocket. From its contents she grabs the tail end of a cigarette and tries to light the pathetic remnant with a lighter that has exhausted itself. Before giving up, a hand reaches out offering her a match. Shocked, she looks expectantly into the face of a young solè wearing a cap that has '275' embroidered on the front. A momentary glimmer of gratefulness flickers beneath her eyes but is quickly replaced with fury and indignation when he drops the match and snatches her bag and sprints across the street. I watch shocked and appalled as she jumps up and screams at him over the cars making their way through the green light. He gives her the finger before running down the street, laughing and jeering, in his brand new pair of Jordan's. She continues to scream, oblivious to the stares of passersby who are unaware that she has just been robbed. Instead, they stare at her with a mingled look of fear and contempt.

I don't know what to do. A stream of 'should I's' rush though my mind. I stand rooted to my spot, undecided as to what to do. Struggling with both a want to help and a fear of how she might react, my decision is made when she looks around resignedly and decides to move on to the next perch.

Later that night, my mother and I continue the argument we've had for the last three months. It has become such a routine event that we have choreographed a somewhat hapless dance in which I pirouette and sashay around her accusatory questions, and she spins with her flailing arms in an attempt to catch and holster me.

My head is pounding. My chest begins to tighten and my breathing becomes loudly audible as it quickens with the heaving rise and fall of my heartbeats. The noise in my ears gets so loud that it manages to block out her yells. She, however, doesn't notice and keeps on at me.

'After everything me and your father been doing for you! All we ask is that you finish your school first. Graduate. Get a good job, and then you can do what you please.' My mother throws herself into one of the chairs and buries her head in her hands in soap-operatic fashion. 'The shame. And of all the people it had to be that Makarita who saw you.' She spits out 'Makarita' like dislodged phlegm. 'Oh, Lord, how can I show my face at church when everyone will know?'

The pounding in my head gets louder, and I silently pray for an aneurism. But I remain standing, and my hand that is clutching the sink counter loosens, and I feel the muscles in my arm slowly untighten. As calmly as I can, I tell my mother that I wasn't doing anything wrong. Yes, I was with him, but we were only at the park having a picnic. *A picnic.* What kind of a picnic was it? Well … it was the kind where we sat on grass, ate some food, drank bottled water, exchanged some words – maybe a few jokes too, said goodbye, then he went one way and I went another way. I have a smart mouth? Well, at least it's smart.

I see her again, her wild curls now tamed beneath a knitted beanie. She wears an oversized T-shirt with the Sydney Harbour Bridge printed on the front. I wonder whether she has been to Sydney, and if she hasn't, why not? What were the circumstances that brought her to where she is now? She smiles and greets a young man in a business suit. He looks embarrassed and quickly side steps her so as to avoid looking at her. She laughs and rubs her hands together, seemingly undisturbed by the young man's rudeness. But I catch a shadow flitter over her face, and I feel the rebuff just as she does.

I am sitting in the courtyard of a busy café. As my friend leans over for another biscotti, I see her across the street rifling through the rubbish bin, searching for something freshly discarded.

'Sad, eh?' my friend whispers sympathetically. Elsewhere in the café and on Lorne Street, no one seems to notice the old woman wearing a T-shirt on a cold August morning. 'Poor thing. I wonder if she has any family.' My friend sips her freshly brewed espresso, and by way of some explanation she adds, 'I guess some people just get unlucky.'

Unlucky. Can it really be that simple that our lives are preordained by a set of chances where you either get the luck of the draw or you miss out? Or are our lives simply determined by the choices we make, and Fate is just the intersection we drive through in deciding which way to turn? What events in her life led her to forage for food in a rubbish bin laden with bacteria and human refuse? A shiver runs through my body as I imagine myself in her position.

I watched a current events show on television a few weeks ago that featured a story about another world that exists beneath our own – the homeless. There were a couple of street kids, runaways from abusive families, who had been shunted from one foster care place to another. They'd had enough and decided to fend for themselves in the many parks, reserves, streets and alleyways of our city.

The story also featured an elderly man in his seventies. He'd been living in the streets for some twenty-odd years. Before that, he used to drive a Mercedes Benz SL500, live in a sprawling hilltop mansion with commanding views of Rangitoto Island and run a successful law and accountancy firm. Through a series of bad judgements, a crippling gambling addiction and improper use of funds, he lost everything in a very public, humiliating way. Dragged through the courts and mercilessly excoriated in the media by angry clients and colleagues whose money he had siphoned, he was bankrupted and jailed for seven years. Now, he slept under bridges or in an available bed in the Mission when the weather became humanly unbearable. He knew where his estranged children lived but had never contacted them, choosing instead to live his life as penance on the very streets he once soared through without a care.

What was the story of the woman with the wild curls? Had her life also been a series of bad judgements or had Fate simply stepped in and delivered her a cruel blow?

My mother and I have not argued for a whole solid week. Or, more correctly, my mother has not spoken to me for a whole week. At first, I welcomed her silence with warm relief. But as the days wear on, I grow anxious and begin to seek any signs of her softening, but I know better. My mother's stubborn streak is legendary in our family. I know I have to make the first attempt to appease the sullen monster that is her stubbornness. So, I wave the white flag by bribing my mother with an offer to buy her a new pair of shoes.

The trip to the mall was a good idea as it has relaxed us both. I miss hearing the warmth in my mother's voice. I miss the tenderness that only a mother and daughter share. The past months have been filled with so much tension that a definite shift in the air is felt the moment you walk into our house. It is my duty as a daughter to acquiesce to my parents' wishes. But for him, this time I won't. He is much too important to me, and for the first time in my life, I am defying my parents.

I am standing in front of a shop window admiring a pair of leather boots when I hear my mother gasp sharply, and in the reflection, I see her shoulders tauten slightly. 'Penina?' I hear the shocked uncertainty in her voice.

Then I hear another voice, belonging to a woman who sounds as though she has not heard that name in a long time. 'Agnes? Is that really you? Oh, my Lord, it is!' She laughs that same deep guttural laugh I have often heard on Queen Street.

I slowly turn and find myself looking at the woman whom I have seen for years roaming the streets of Auckland city. Her hair is still as wild and as untamed. Stunned, I look from my mother to the woman, who obviously know each other, but how?

'Penina, o a mai oe? Where are you staying?' I see my mother's eyes quickly take in Penina's appearance, and I can tell by her stance and her tone that she is affected.

'Oh, I still have my flat in Freemans Bay.' She digs her hands into her pockets, and I can tell she is anxious to leave.

'Penina ... are you okay ...?' My mother's voice trails off. She is unsure of what to say next.

She gives that thick, rough laugh. 'Of course, eh, you take care okay, suga.' With a flick of her hand she saunters away from us, pulling her frayed cardigan tightly around herself.

Still stunned, I look at my mother and breathlessly ask her how she knows Penina. *Penina?* Pearl. And she spoke in Samoan.

On the way to the car my mother tells me that Penina and she had been friends in the same village when they were young. Growing up, Penina had blossomed into a beautiful young woman who soon caught the eye of a rich palagi, but not just a palagi – an American. Everyone in her family, including her village, was happily envious of her. She had attained respectability and social standing amongst the foreigners who were arriving in droves to Stevenson's idyllic shores. The ideal didn't last, however, when the American grew tired of Penina and returned to America with their daughter. Unable to cope with the humiliation and the heartbreaking anguish caused by the loss of her child, Penina suffered a nervous breakdown and was brought to New Zealand by her parents. It seems she never did get over her loss.

I recognised the look in my mother's eyes when she recounted the sad story. It was the look in the eyes of every mother who desperately wants only the very best for their child. And immediately, I understood the tense months of strained conversations and frustrated tears. I understood finally that her fears were warranted from mere love and concern and not some parental need for dominance. Wordlessly, we get into the car, and with my own eyes, I let my mother know that I will be okay. She squeezes my hand in return, and we have come to a silent understanding.

I think about Penina and the sufferings she must have surely endured – the pain of losing your child, and thus ultimately yourself, as it is the extension of your soul and the right to all your wrongs. To look at a lone figure all you see is their outward appearance – just another person in a crowd. Yet embodied in this simple figure is a history of encounters, a history of people they have known, seen, let into their lives and places that they have lived in, visited, passed through. I look at a seven-year-old and think about all that they will see and experience, and I look at a seventy-one-year-old and wonder about what they have seen and experienced. You can open a book and turn the pages until you reach the end. But you can sit down and talk with, say, your mother and realise that there are simply not enough pages to fill her life story.

'Hey, are you okay, baby?' I turn and look at him and smile. Kissing the top of his blond hair, I tell him, yes, I am okay.

Nuku-tu-taha

Zora Feilo-Makapa

Nuku-tu-taha
Wild and free as a bird
You stand alone in the blue Pacific
Your rocky coral reef with its jagged edges
You are a contradiction to idyllic sandy isles
As you are mother and father – nurturer and protector
The sun and the moon
The sky and the ocean

Years have passed since the Captain tried to anchor
Seeking to be your discoverer
But you rebelled for protection against all things foreign
They were not to understand this simplicity
Forever condemning you and your children
To the name Savage Island

Your sons and daughters have travelled afar
Yet you always stand firm
They still declare you as their own
You are not worried as parents do not forget their children
You trust in them faithfully
And Tagaloa who will bring them back home

I am your child Nuku-tu-taha
And I want you to be proud of me
Wherever I go I take you in my heart

And I share you with the world
For my love for you is immense
And I cry when I hear your name

Nuku-tu-taha is an old name for Niue Island. It means the island
that stands alone.

The Vaka

Zora Feilo-Makapa

You carved me of wood and put me to sea to travel the oceans wide.
I have brought the people across the Pacific to these places they call home.

My long paddles were used by the strongest of warriors with their able arms of steel. We came across the magnificent blue seas with navigators seeking a new destination. A never-ending quest of seeing beyond the horizon with the families I hold dearly in my care.

In the spirit of my forefathers, I will bring them safely to brand new shores.
A place where the corals of the ocean harbour a thousand different mysteries.

The waves crash upon us, but they just make you stronger.
My children navigate the stars in the darkness. In this time of adversity it helps keep your vision focused, for I am here to help you reach your destiny.

The wind is howling as the rain falls. We are rocking in the ocean.
The children are hungry, the children are crying, but there is no turning back.

There is a place for us in this glorious Pacific, and we seek it out.
Our spirit leads us, and Tagaloa guides us and keeps us safe.
And so it is we carry on.

The sun shines, the waters are sparkling.
You swim to catch the fish that are needed to nourish your bodies
to continue the journey that keeps you strengthened.
I watch as you speak in my mother tongue. I am fascinated by you,
and I am alive with your spirit, as my body is your vessel.

I have watched you face the torrential weather hurling around
you.
The pouring rain, the thunderous skies, bolts of lightening and the
pounding unforgiving seas – and still you never give up.

You are unwavering in your desire to lead our people courageously
across this expansive ocean. I am humbled to be a part of your
pioneering quest as Hawaiiki is the place we left behind.

For your children
And your children's children.

I am the journey
I am the vaka.

The Red Socks

Afshana Ali and Elenoa Tamani

The banging woke her up.

Blinking, she looked around. A brown door, with its paint peeling, slowly came into focus. The banging was coming from behind it.

'What ...?' she thought blurrily. She had been living in silence for so long that the loud noise was a shock, penetrating her unconsciousness. She tried to turn her head, but the blinding pain stopped her.

'Where am I?' The banging continued. Someone was saying something. The words were indistinguishable from the pounding of fists on the door. There was an urgency behind it, but she felt too tired to pay attention to it. Slowly, painfully she turned to one side. Two grotesque stumps of red were where her hands used to be.

'Radhika!' the voice said.

'Yes,' she whispered from a parched and scratchy throat.

'Where's my socks?' the voice said.

'Socks?' Radhika thought hazily.

The question was impatiently repeated.

It was too much effort to think. Her eyes re-focused on the red things in front of her.

'Red,' Radhika thought. Her mind could not move beyond that. Images flicked through her mind ... red sarees, red sindhur, red decorations, red flowers and the mesmerising image of flickering red flames. They were significant to her, but the effort was too much for her, so she whirled back into the awaiting darkness.

Another sound, fainter but insistent, stirred Radhika into wakefulness. She tried opening her eyes, but her eyelids weighed a ton. The brown peeling door and the seemingly endless pool of red swam lazily into view.

Radhika felt exhausted, but the noise caught her attention again. Slowly and painfully, she turned her head towards it. It came from something round with marks in it. Her mind finally made the connection. A clock.

Turning on her back brought spasms of pain hissing out of her mouth. The pain seemed to be coming from her hands. It fixed her attention and fleetingly cleared her mind from the haze surrounding it. She seemed to be lying on something soft. A mattress.

'What happened to my hands?' Radhika wondered. She glanced furtively towards them. They appeared to be attached to a pool of red. It seemed too much of an effort to unravel this mystery.

Slowly other sounds penetrated – the ticking of the clock, a steady puttering of rain on the roof and the whooshing of cars.

'What am I doing here?' she pondered tiredly. A bang on the door startled her.

'Radhika, where are my socks?' the bang cried.

Like water let loose from a closed-up dam, everything came rushing back to her ….

She had got up to prepare breakfast and lunch for her husband. Then she had gone into the spare bedroom and locked the door. The room had been dark except for the dim light struggling through the curtains. She had stared at herself in the mirror. It had reflected a brown-skinned, black-eyed girl with the normal accessories of hair, nose, ears and mouth. Nobody exceptional. There were no wrinkles, but there were dark circles under her eyes, so it was hard to gauge her age.

Radhika had gazed at the girl in the mirror, and bringing her hands in front of her, she had placed them on the mirror so that they had covered all of her face except for her eyes. The black and brown irises of the eyes had stared back at her. The little streams of light in the room had not reflected in the eyes. There had been no life in them.

Radhika had stared at the eyes and remembered the other times she had done the same thing. She had been seven when she had first noticed that the ring around the centre of her eyes was brown. So excited by the discovery, she had rushed off to tell everyone. For a whole month after that she had checked her eyes every morning to make sure that the brown ring had not disappeared overnight, much to her parents' amusement.

When Radhika had been ten and her elder sister, Rani, had showed her how to put kohl around her eyes, she had noticed it again. The kohl had highlighted her eyes, lending them an air of mystery. But more importantly, her sister had told her about the light in the eyes.

Radhika had scoffed. 'How could there be light in the eyes? They aren't flashlights,' she had protested.

'It isn't that, you dummy!' Rani had exclaimed. 'Have you noticed that babies' eyes sparkle with light?' she had asked.

'Yes. So do mine give out light also?' she had asked.

'Yes. The light reflects the life within,' Rani had replied. Radhika had pondered on that for a while. 'But Grandma's eyes aren't so bright,' she had said.

Rani had nodded in agreement. 'That's because Grandma doesn't have long to live, so the light of life within her is dying.'

'What should we do' Radhika had whispered, becoming frightened.

'There's nothing we can do about it, it's the circle of life,' Rani had sadly replied. 'But you, my little munchkin, don't have to worry because you've a long life ahead of you, so your eyes will give out light for a long time.'

Radhika had been twelve when her grandma had died. She remembered visiting her grandma in the hospital, connected to lots of wires and machines. It had frightened Radhika to see her grandma like that. She had crept to the bed and slowly kissed

Grandma's wrinkled cheeks. Grandma had opened her eyes and smiled a bit. Radhika had gazed into her eyes and had seen the dimming light of life. Grandma had died while sleeping that night.

Radhika's mind flicked back to when she was fifteen. She had gazed in the mirror seeing herself for the first time as an adult in a saree. It had been at Rani's wedding and everything had been so thrilling. Her eyes had sparkled not only with excitement but also with the kohl and the sparkly dust on her eyelids. But they had filled with tears when the groom took Rani away.

The next time Radhika had gazed into her eyes, they had again been filled with tears. Her parents had just told her that they had arranged a marriage for her. She had turned eighteen and just finished high school. She had protested until she had been hoarse, but it had been in vain.

'The marriage is very advantageous because the boy is from overseas,' her parents had told Radhika firmly. 'This will make your future.'

'But I don't want to go overseas or marry,' Radhika had protested. 'I want to study, work and travel a bit.'

'It's the responsibility of the parents to make sure that when their daughter reaches a certain age, she marries,' her parents had explained. 'You can't move out and work in the city or travel alone. What will other people think? That we can't provide for you? Look what happened to Sadhana's parents when they gave her all that freedom. They'll never be able to show their faces again in society after she ran away with that white boy.'

'But they were in love,' Radhika had whispered, tears dripping slowly down her face.

'Love, bah!' her mother had exclaimed. 'Where was her love for the parents? After all the years and money they spent on her, how does she pay them back? Trust me, that marriage won't work. They're from two different cultures and religions. I heard last week that she's even going to church with him. What about their children? What will they be? They're now dead to the family. We know what's best for you.'

The marriage had passed in a daze for Radhika. She had vaguely known that she had said and done what was expected, but her only memories were of a haze of red. Radhika's husband had left her alone soon after the marriage to wait for the visa. She had committed to memory the image of herself in the little mirror of her bedroom on the day she left the country.

It had rained the day she had arrived, just like it was raining now. She turned her head to the window. The rain seemed to be lashing more fiercely now as if to combat her memories. On her arrival, she had been bombarded with new sights, smells, sounds and colours. Her husband had picked her up and showed her around the little two-bedroom flat that he had rented in the suburbs. For the first time in months, she had felt alive and hopeful of new adventures.

Her husband had explained that he worked day shifts at a supermarket and night shifts in a factory. Radhika had asked if she could work also and had been overjoyed when he had agreed. After settling in, she had started applying for jobs. At first, she had been optimistic as employment agencies had assured her that with her qualifications she could get a job easily. But gradually, the rejections had come pouring through, and she became disheartened. With her husband not home most days, family and friends being so far away, Radhika had found it difficult to cope.

Eventually, she had been given the job of packing shelves at the nearest supermarket. She had made some friends and started feeling hopeful that, with a little experience, she would be able to get something better. But now, Radhika rarely saw her husband as her hours were mainly during the weekends.

The year passed slowly, and things remained the same. She began the second year with a feeling of despair. Radhika had found her husband's clothing smelling of perfume. She did not know what to do. Her feelings of rejection grew.

Summer passed into winter – gloomy, cold and dreary. Radhika's feeling of encroaching darkness grew.

Yesterday, Radhika had come home and started dinner. Turning on the gas stove, the flames had burst out. She had just stood there, mesmerised by the reddish orange flames.

'So easy,' she had thought, 'and so beautiful.' The flames had seemed hungry to her, ready to devour anything. She had swayed nearer to the flames, but the strident ring of the phone had broken her trance. Radhika had turned around and tried to locate the phone. Just as she was about to pick it up, it had stopped ringing. She had turned back to the flames, but they had lost their allure.

'Dinner. I'm making dinner,' Radhika had remembered. Afterwards, she had lain on the couch and turned on the TV. After surfing the channels and finding nothing interesting, she had gazed dispiritedly at the blank screen. The darkness had felt so near to her and comforting that she had given in to it.

It had been her husband, coming back from his night shift, who had shaken Radhika awake. She had been disorientated and groggy. She had struggled to the bedroom and collapsed on the bed. After his dinner, her husband had showered and fallen asleep next to her. The sounds of snoring had soon pervaded the room.

'Is this what my life's going to be like?' Radhika had asked herself. Thoughts had kept revolving until she had started to feel angry – at herself, at life, at everyone. She had gone to the living room and started ripping all the clothes in the hamper. Radhika's anger had given her momentum. Shredded pieces of cloth now lay round her. Miserable and her anger spent, her bones creaking like an old woman's, she had slowly got up, gathered all the pieces together and stuffed them in the trash. Making her way slowly to the bedroom, she had lain next to her husband. Feelings of despair had yet again overwhelmed her, but with her anger spent, she had slept fitfully.

The beeping of the alarm clock had woken Radhika this morning. Opening her eyes, she had beheld only darkness weighing in on her. Like a robot, Radhika had gone through her normal routine of making breakfast and lunch. Still in the same trance, she had gone to the second bedroom, locking the door with a loud click.

For a long time, Radhika had sat on the bed and stared at her eyes in the mirror. Slowly, she had opened the little side drawer and taken out a small knife. Staring at it fixedly, she had gently placed the knife on her wrist and slit it lightly. Blood had started dripping. Moving the knife to the other hand, she had done the same thing. Staring at the blood dripping leisurely, she had wondered dazedly why it wasn't black.

Radhika had begun to feel lightheaded and, closing her eyes, had lain back dizzily but peacefully.

More banging jostled her out of her reverie.

'Where's my socks?' it shouted. Radhika looked around. There was a cupboard of her husband's clothes in this bedroom.

Taking care not to jolt her hands, Radhika got up painfully. Her mind whirled, and she felt like vomiting. Swallowing hard and breathing heavily through sheer force of will, she took one step at a time towards the cupboard, nudged the door and grabbed a towel. Grimacing with pain, she wrapped it around her wrists. It was enough so that she could grab, with her bloody hands, the pair of white socks that lay on the shelf.

Unlocking the door took some time. Outside, she saw her husband muttering and flinging clothes everywhere.

She shuffled to him and whispered, 'Your socks'.

Her husband stopped abruptly and turned, frowning heavily. Spying the socks in her hand, he shouted, 'I don't want red socks. Where's my white socks? Didn't you do the laundry yesterday?'

Feeling her strength fading fast, Radhika limped over to the bed and sat down heavily. With her head hanging down, she said, 'I don't know.'

'What do you mean you don't know?' he demanded. 'No matter, I'm going to be late. I'll have to wear these.' He snatched them from her.

'Aagh, these are wet! Where are the ones I wore yesterday?' Angrily, he rummaged in the dirty laundry basket for his socks, put them on along with his boots and strode out the front door, banging it loudly behind him.

Radhika sat in silence for a while. Sounds whirled around in the background but did not penetrate her consciousness. Bewildered and sad, she limped agonisingly to the bathroom.

The bright glare of the bathroom light blinded her momentarily. Her hands were emblazoned in fiery crimson. Covering the lower part of her face, she stared directly into the mirror. Gazing back at her were two dark pools that seemed to be absorbing the light.

Inhaling a quick, harsh breath, she noticed that the brown in her eyes had disappeared. The irises were completely black. Turning to the sink, she washed the blood off her hands, bandaged them, changed into clean clothes and walked into the bedroom. Spying the red socks on the bed, she threw them into the trash. Grabbing her bag, she slowly walked to the door and closed it gently behind her.

It was Saturday. Another day at work.

Statement from the baddies

Tusiata Avia

You are the blood-stained patient
Yes, you are the blind man standing by the roadside
You are the crippled child

The tragically widowed, pregnant woman
The Russian circus elephant
And the Indian houseboy.

Me? (Do I even need to say what I am?)
I suppose I am the hangars for the Israeli air force
The thigh high boot on Condoleezza's right leg

I would be at least ten percent of CO_2 emissions
And very probably the fiancé (or at the very least the lifelong
    friend)
Of Robert Mugabi's youngest daughter.

I think that makes it clear where we stand
Who gets to nail who
And who had better get used to the idea of everlasting darkness.

Nafanua and the religious police

Tusiata Avia

There is a name for them
the religious police
who come looking for you

when you've done something wrong.
They hit women with batons
around the ankles if their socks have slipped.

They come to her house and she knows they have seen her
or the neighbours have
through the window

bent over
her head in his lap.
She runs into the market and they chase her

with swords like the moon
and it's like running in Damascus over cobblestones of glass.
She loses them in the sweet shop

she buys syrup cakes
big huge ones
and drives them into her mouth like thunderbolts.

Wind

Tusiata Avia

She's crossing the street and there are two little blonde girls
either side of their mother and one of them is screaming
something (later she thinks it was probably *Ooo yuck*)
the mother says *No she's beautiful*
she's a Sa-mo-wan, you know Sa-mo-wan, we have one at the back
she looks down at the girl and smiles
Are you looking at what I look like?
the child leans into her mother's waist
and looks at her as if she's thrown sand in her eyes and is pleased
and is safe. As they round the corner the mother says
Don't you ever let me
and the rest is taken away by the wind.

There Was
Never Silence

Tanielu de Mollard

(A Genealogy)

When I first saw you it was like ... concrete.
The way you were covered with grey. Hanging
around under your eyes and slicking your hair down.
And a neck you could just slit. *The Colour Grey* – they
should write a book about it. When feeling refused us and
our feet couldn't reach the ground. We mounded promises
like   glistening laws about us – pale and sturdy, yet unfulfilled.

Rereading your letter leaves an aftertaste of incorrect grammar.
(So young) was uttered repeatedly: (So young) (So young) (So
young).

That was when we knew everything. It was with great ease
that we were certain then. For example: many people were very
sad or very tired and it tiptoed around backstage, behind their low
quiet words (later sounding fast and mythological) and methodical
executions.

The church was as tight-lipped and firm jawed as you might
remember. (Share a secret) it whispered. And then covered its tracks
by implying (Don't ask) (Don't tell) in a stare. That was when I
went back the other day to sit in its garden and smoke alone. And
listen to the shapes of trees.

But I don't trust nature.
I'm not like you. We knew these people were old.
And that we were new.

.I wrote a letter to Edward while I was there. I was thinking of asking if I could call him something that sounds better but I didn't. Sushi has become my favourite food, I think. I never feel bloated afterwards, but I feel very uncivilised not knowing how to use chopsticks. Becoming invisible isn't difficult here. When knowing everything discontinued for us we felt: (unsure) (afraid) (abnormal). And when we felt this we bathed regularly. We were always cleaning or cleansing then because we felt we looked like dirt.

Now that *feeling* was an inundation, we learnt to do things.

When we learnt to make excellent scones. (So young) was said again (So young). And you had a neck.
You could just – *slice.*

There's an apple core on the bench opposite me, and it's going brown. Underneath the bench next to it is some mince-and-cheese (fallen from its pie). A couple sits on this bench in love: legs touching fingers touching sleeves. I feel like a dick sitting in front of them with chicken fat under my nails and grease on my mouth. Oh yeah, by the way, I'm eating (animals) again.

But even the most excellent of scones leave something to be desired. They lack in flair and dedication, occupying valuable space whilst offering little in return. A scone does not declare its intentions, refusing any clear commitment. Last night, I asked Edward if he was a (religious man). I'm not sure, but maybe I was trying to flirt with him: (—man) balanced awkwardly at the tip of the sentence, but it felt nice. Although it's perfectly natural to be one, I suspect it'll never really happen for me. At least he can pronounce my name, even if he'll never understand its meaning.

Scones are irreligious and selfish (and in this world of ours there have been so many scones).

★★★★★★

Seeing you: Ethereal (dressed liked that in your concrete shroud). I wanted to dig you up and plant you in a window box. But you know I'd never do it. We all know I'd never.

Disappointment was shaming, and when we bathed (regularly) we wished to glisten. Something that glistens is a fake pearl on a wedding dress. When we wore it we did not require knowledge of anything. We longed for delicious things: vanilla ice cream, meringues, boiled eggs, etc.

I wrote (I love you) once, at the bottom of a letter. But I ripped it off before I gave it to you. I just wanted to know how that would feel. Like the temptation to thread. A blade through your throat. Once when I answered the phone (Dear Heavenly Father) just came out automatically. And we never had lunchboxes, only shitty plastic bags. And sometimes we were deceived by sandwiches: white on top but brown underneath.

Tonight, I plan to drink until my mind and body sing. In unison and in harmony and in discord. I want to spew words and feel emotional. I'll probably flirt with Edward again, and we'll probably pretend it never happened. I don't mind. He is a dick, but I like him. Without saying it, I think we understand that each of us is the only one who entirely believes the other's stories.

(   ) was a constant concern during that
period. Thankfully, we knew the difference between wrong and
it was right to bathe regularly and glisten (baking excellent scones)
at a higher frequency of right-doings made us better than relatives
who made poor-quality scones or, worse still, did not know how
to make a scone whatsoever.
In the first
place.

While truanting class, I watch people drift like clouds: (fr)agile
(tired) (beautiful) people. Wind-like people. Tree-branch (sky and
fluid) and sometimes concrete people. Visible people too. Like the
girl who never lifts her head and once pretended. Eating yoghurt
proved a near-impossibility given their unfamiliarity with utensils.
People are cups of flour (decks of cards), piles of humming stones.
Their fingers must always have been dirty and whether bathing
(for them) occurred often or seldom it is difficult to ascertain.

Your aftermath is like sitting inside a needle. Like the bridging
ocean I can admire but cannot hope to comprehend.

You pushed past me on the stair saying (scuse bro) which is
something you'd never say. (So young) was never uttered. (Too
young) was mentioned much later.
But much later we knew much (much) less.

Tatau

Philomena Lee

Give me the depth to who I am
Don't ask me to give you identity because
I know where I belong, and who I am
Be strong!
Know who you are before you come to me
I can make you stronger but I can't make you.
You can be what I am, by knowing who you are.
Just don't rely on me to tell you where you belong
I have travelled through space and time
with Taeme and Tilafaiga and have left my mark on many.
I take with me the language and the land
I am fa'a Samoa
So wear me with pride and treat me with the dignity that I am
Do not abuse me as statement, but honour the statement in me
Come to me at the end of your journey, so I can cloak you with
Strength and dignity
Don't seek me at the beginning because
I will add to your confusion.

Devotion

Philomena Lee

He strides with purpose through the streets of Apia
I look, but not to see, for my own safety.
He wears his poverty around his loins
showing remnants of what was once a lavalava
As he walks through the town, tall and lean
probably from the great distances walked in bare feet
His face is tidy but unshaven
His greying hair is combed but uncut
I wondered where he was headed in great strides.
Two days later I saw him again as I was resting from the
Heat of the sun, and in front of the cathedral
He strode past me to his destination
He reached the doors of the inner sanctum
As he stooped to bow, he modestly tried
to lengthen his loincloth in an act of reverence
He stays a while praying then rises, backs out, turns and
Within three steps he is striding past me and away.

The Islander

Naila Fanene

'Open your desks!' Sister Anne bellowed from the front of the room. Her steely, cold eyes were fixed firmly on Malia.

'Oh, oh, the hunchback's on the warpath again,' Jane Johnson lisped in a high-pitched squeal, 'and she's heading for that dark girl down the back'. Malia was the only 'dark' girl in the class.

Sister Anne's masculine frame rocked from side to side down the narrow aisle towards the vicinity of Malia's desk. Her beady eyes narrowed, like those of a predator about to pounce on its prey. 'Ugh, what a witch'. Malia cringed in silent terror.

'You, what's your name?' Malia had been in Sister Anne's class for a whole month now.

'Malia Sefulu-Vai, Sister,' Malia responded, eyes downcast as Sister Anne hovered over her desk, all the while glaring down at the frightened ten-year-old.

'What sort of a name is that?' she sneered.

'It's Samoan, Sister.' Malia was proud of her name, which she'd inherited from both her aunt and grandmother. 'But my English name's Mary.' The apology in Malia's voice was unmistakable.

'Then why didn't you say so in the first place?' the old nun croaked hoarsely. 'I can't pronounce that other name.'

'You mean you won't.' Malia could feel a burning rage surging within her young belly. She was angry at herself for not having the courage to speak up for her aunt and her grandmother.

'Why don't they have normal names like ours?' Joan Hoggett, who sat across from Malia, mumbled just loud enough for Malia to hear. Nothing about Malia was normal to her white classmates or to Sister Anne.

The old nun lowered her voice. Her menacing tone sparked a renewed uneasiness in the pit of Malia's stomach. 'Anya's blue fountain pen's missing'. Her eyes rested firmly on Malia. 'When did you notice your pen missing, Anya?' The sick charade continued.

'This morning after play, Sister,' Anya squealed politely. Malia never squealed or shrieked at the top of her lungs like some of the other girls in her class, but somehow 'white' voices didn't offend Sister Anne. Malia's voice did.

Anya was one of several students in the class whom Sister Anne openly indulged. This select group included Olga the Croatian brainbox, Joan and Barbara, who openly flaunted their dubious reputation of being the local 'bikes' and Jane Johnson, whose parents were upstanding pillars of the community.

Joan and Barbara, who were both thirteen and still at primary school, gave free lessons on boys and sex around the milk crate every Monday morning. The salacious, spiced-up details of their weekend exploits shocked even the most liberated palate among their curious audience of eleven- and twelve-year-olds. Mortal sin and the threat of hell didn't bother Barbara and Joan. They wanted a good time, and they wanted it now. Even Sister Anne knew better than to push their uncouth buttons. In fact, nobody dared to stand up to Barbara and Joan.

Jane Johnson, on the other hand, had the perfect family. Her father was a successful businessman and an active member of almost every committee in the parish, and her mother was always involved with fund-raising for the school and parish. Jane, however, was a nondescript, bland individual whose pan-white face, crust-speckled, red-rimmed eyes and annoying lisp belied her real qualities. When Jane had something to say, she didn't speak, she whined. But Jane knew how to play Sister Anne. And the old nun treated Jane as her intellectual equal. She listened attentively to whatever Jane had to say. She laughed along with the rest of the class at Jane's funny stories that abounded during class lessons. And despite the fact that much of what Jane said was utter tripe, she was given plenty of air time by Sister Anne.

Ten year old Malia, with her brown skin and working-class, Island background, was conspicuously outnumbered in this white, middle-class Catholic girls' school. Malia's parents didn't work in an office or own a business like the parents of her white classmates; they were shift workers who worked long hours in a factory. Furthermore, her parents spoke Samoan to her at home, not English like the parents of her white classmates.

Malia's classmates saved the 'best' of themselves for the cooking bus each week. Joan Hoggett was always the first to start the ball rolling. 'My boyfriend said there are too many bungas in New Zealand.'

'Yeah,' echoed her offsider, Barbara Cress.

Jane Johnson joined in with her own dose of venom for people she didn't particularly like. 'Well, my mother said we should send all these coconuts back to where they belong because they can't speak English properly, and they get into too many fights when they've been drinking.'

'Yeah,' echoed Barbara. Jane's diatribe of insults had only just begun.

'My parents were going to send me to Senior Grammar, but they've changed their minds because there are too many horis and coconuts there now. I'm going to St Catherine's instead. At least all the kids there are white like us.'

There was only so much of Jane Johnson's snootiness that her rival Joan Hogget could stand before she'd re-assert her rightful position again as the leader of the group. 'Me and my boyfriend did it on the back seat of his friend's car on Saturday night at the Speedways,' she screeched. Bullfrog eyes had everyone's attention back again. But only a select few on the bus were privy to the 'delectable' details of her sexual encounters.

The sting from these insults seeped into the very core of Malia's soul. She was now convinced that being 'different' and 'brown' was the worst possible fate to befall anyone.

'Hey, Malia, or whatever your name is,' Joan would screech from the back of the bus, 'how do you say coconut in your language?'

'Don't know,' Malia would lie. 'I can't speak Samoan.'

'Why not?' Joan had a habit of hissing through her teeth at you if you were 'different'. 'You're a coconut, aren't you?'

A chorus of high-pitched, triumphant shrieks cheered Joan on as Malia withdrew, defeated once again, into her invisible, brown shell.

Amanda Brown, who usually sat behind Malia on the bus, did not join in the 'fun'. Amanda was short and stocky with thick, short-cropped hair and a face that was a blot of ginger freckles. In fact, Amanda could easily have passed for a boy. 'Malia, you don't look like a typical Islander. You know, you're actually pretty for an Islander,' Amanda whispered into Malia's neck. This backhanded compliment was the nicest thing anyone had ever said to Malia on the cooking bus. It could only have come from someone who was herself 'different'. Malia needed to feel good about herself. It had been a long day.

'What is a "typical" Islander, Amanda?' the naïve young Samoan whispered.

'Um, I don't really know. You're the first Islander I've ever met.' Amanda shrugged her shoulders and buried her head again in her book.

The class now closed ranks in the hunt for the culprit who had stolen Anya's pen. The silence was deafening as the lid of each desk flipped open in unison. Sister Anne had bypassed all the 'white' desks. With every squish of her rubber-soled shoes, the cramps in Malia's stomach intensified.

'Where's Anya's fountain pen?' the old nun demanded, elbows akimbo. Malia tightened her stomach muscles in defiance.

'I don't know.' Her voice was steady as she forced back tears of indignation and shame.

Accusing eyes, devoid of human compassion, bore down on Malia's drooping shoulders. 'Empty out your desk!' The old nun spat out her words as she tossed Malia's textbooks, her exercise books and all her pens and pencils willy-nilly across the floor.

'I didn't take Anya's pen,' Malia protested quietly. But, her pleas fell on Sister Anne's deaf ears.

'Where's Anya's pen?' the old nun insisted. The whites of her grey, lifeless eyes were now blood red with rage. Malia stood her ground, fighting back the tears as she looked down at her now-empty desk. Anya's pen was nowhere to be found. The old nun slammed Malia's desk shut. 'You find Anya's pen and bring it to me tomorrow morning before school or else!' she shrieked, jabbing her crooked finger into the side of Malia's face.

'That's if I come back to this bloody school again, you old hag.' Malia swallowed hard before she could open her mouth to speak. Sister Anne turned and walked back to the front of the room without stopping to inspect any of the 'white' desks on her way. Why would she? Malia was the only Islander in the class, and white girls don't steal.

Suddenly, Anya's angelic squeal pierced through the uneasy muttering in the room. 'Look.' She held up her fountain pen for all to see. 'I've found my pen.'

'Where was it?' Joan enquired, annoyed that Anya had owned up about her pen before Sister Anne could sink her claws into that dark girl again the next day.

'Right here inside my English book,' Anya confessed with a sheepish grin.

Sister Anne smiled approvingly at Anya. 'Please stand for prayers, girls.' With her right hand about to make the sign of the cross, Sister Anne roared at Malia once more. 'You! Down the back!' Malia heaved yet again with embarrassment. 'Make sure you tidy up your books before you leave this afternoon.' No apology from Sister Anne. No apology from Anya.

Malia looked at her books strewn over the floor at the back of the room. And as she gathered her things together, she repeated Sister Anne's mantra one more time to herself before leaving her class. 'All people, black, white, brown, yellow and red are equal in the sight of God.'

Eti's Dilemma

Naila Fanene

Sala stepped gingerly from the gangplank onto terra firma. It was May 1953 when the *Tofua* dispatched her human cargo at Princess Wharf. We edged our way slowly forward as the howling south-westerly lashed against our frail bodies mercilessly. Glancing back over her shoulder towards the dark, ubiquitous horizon, Sala thanked her God for carrying us safely to Papa and to our new life in New Zealand. Papa had been away from us now for almost two years.

Out of nowhere, Papa suddenly appeared, tears of euphoria streaming down his handsome face. The sight of us all barefoot and dressed only in light, cotton clothing distracted him, but only for a moment. 'Where's all the money I sent you to buy the children warm clothes and shoes for their trip to New Zealand?' His voice was barely audible. Sala remained silent, clutching Mina tightly.

Papa pointed to a black Chevrolet parked just outside the main gate. 'Quickly, into the car. All of you'. Finally, we pulled up outside an old two-storey, wooden house, fronted by staid oak trees with thick, crooked branches. Both sides of the long, dark street were crammed with dingy houses and punctuated now and again by a dimly lit street lamp. 'We've arrived!' The feigned delight in Papa's voice did little to cheer us up.

'A o fea e gofo ai ia Mama?' ('Where does Mama live?') Eleven-year-old Lita enquired nervously.

'Mama's room is at the top of the stairs. That's where you'll be sleeping, Lita, with Mama.' The tone in Papa's voice signaled an end to the discussion about his mother. Tears filled Lita's long, slender eyes. It hurt Papa to see Lita upset, but his mother's needs always came first. Papa's voice mellowed a little. 'There's only enough room downstairs for Sala and the younger children, Lita.'

Then it was Sala's turn. 'Eti, o ai le la fafige palagi?' ('Eti, who's that European woman?') It was no secret that Papa and his brothers, Paul and Philip, had a penchant for palagi women.

'That's Mrs Mayne, the landlady.'

Any fears that Sala might have harboured about her husband having an affair with this woman were immediately dispelled after a closer inspection of Mrs Mayne's face. It was a map of heavily indented wrinkles. Her eyes peered out at Sala from under heavy folds of sagging skin hanging loosely over each eyelid and Mrs Mayne's tightly pursed, paper-thin, lips were heavily smeared with thick, red lipstick.

She ignored Sala altogether. 'Eti, I've already told you. Your wife and children aren't welcome here.' The tone in Mrs Mayne's voice reignited that sick feeling in the pit of Sala's belly. Papa just smiled at her. 'If immigration finds out you've got five children and a wife stashed away in one of my bedrooms, I could get into a lot of trouble.' She waved her finger at Papa. 'I don't want any trouble with immigration, do you hear?'

Papa beckoned us to follow him to our room.

The stench of neglect and loneliness exploded through the bedroom door as Papa thrust it open. Except for an old double bed with a kapok mattress, covered over by a grey blanket, tattered and torn, which sagged in the middle all the way to the floor, the room was void of any real furniture. 'That's your bed.' Papa's eyes rested first on eight-year-old Etuati and then on Peka and me.' The heaviness in Papa's voice clouded the thick, stagnant air. The second kapok mattress, urine stained and filthy with grime, sprawled out on the floor at the foot of the double bed was Papa and Sala's bed. Mina's freshly painted, wooden cot, which was tucked away behind the door, was the only real spark of life in the dismal, grey room.

'E fai fo'i kakou mea ai i kokogu le poku?' ('Do we cook and eat in the room as well?') Sala suddenly remembered that we hadn't eaten anything for several hours. Papa bent down on all fours and from underneath Mina's cot dragged out his 'kitchen', which consisted of a few tin cups and plates, one or two pots and pans and a handful of cutlery. He rustled up a delicious meal on his small kerosene stove in next to no time. Papa cooked and ate his meals alone in his room but not tonight.

'Oi, Eti, o fea le mea e fai ai kaga mea?' ('Um, Eti, where do you do the washing?'). Sala's dark eyes scanned the room yet again as she gobbled down Papa's special treat, which the Chinese cooks in his aunt's restaurant back in Samoa had taught him to make.

'Sala, you'll have to do Mama's washing together with ours,' Eti ordered.

'Why?' Sala was hoping that she and Eti could start afresh without his interfering mother.

'Because Ruby's too busy working overtime,' he lied.

'E le'o a'u o se kavigi o lou kiga, Eti. Fai i lou kiga e ku'u le ula ula pe'a ua ma'i.' ('I'm not your mother's servant, Eti. If she's so sick, tell her to stop smoking.') Sala stopped eating and pushed her plate to one side. Mama was Ruby's mother not hers.

As we tiptoed down the passageway behind Papa, the rancid odour of stale cigarettes and cheap perfume oozed from the pores of unwashed bodies that watched us furtively through the slits of their doors left slightly ajar. The door to the wash-house was hanging off its rusty hinges. The concrete floor was cold and hard under our bare feet and the copper tub was half filled with putrid-smelling water that had turned stagnant. Papa pointed to the two grey concrete tubs. 'You can bathe the children there, Sala.' Sala ignored the sharp pangs of regret that gnawed away at her each time she heard the horn of a ship leaving port.

Two weeks passed by without incident. Each morning, Lita would sneak downstairs and snuggle into bed with Peka and me as soon as she had emptied Mama's pee pot. Sala cooked Mama's meals and washed the phlegm-filled rags that the old woman had spat into. Papa's brothers, Paul and Philip, would not hear of their palagi wives helping Sala with Mama's cooking and washing. Then on the Monday morning of our third week at the boarding house, we awoke to the pounding of heavy fists on our bedroom door.

'Immigration! Open up!' Papa opened the door to a barrage of questions.

'Are you Etuati Marks?' the younger of the two men asked. Papa nodded. 'Do you speak English?'

'Yes,' Papa's retorted gruffly.

'Are you living in this one room with your wife and five children?' The young officer poked his head around Papa. We were all sitting upright in our bed. 'Do you know that's against the law?' He shook his head disapprovingly as his voice droned on. 'This is a boarding house for single adults. And, your three older children should not be sleeping in the same room as you and your wife. Now, Mr Marks, you either find a bigger place for your wife and children to shift into by the end of next week, or they will be deported to Samoa.'

Eti stopped off at the Prince of Wales after work that day for a beer. 'Go and see Father Emilio,' Simi insisted. 'He'll know what to do.' Simi McDonald and Eti had been friends since their school days at Marist Boys School in Apia. They had both married village girls and had traveled together to New Zealand on the *Matua*.

The German priest, Father Emilio, knew Papa's family well. He listened intently as Papa poured his heart out.

'There's a Catholic orphanage in Howick where your daughters can stay for as long as they need to while you and Sala save up for a deposit. Etuati can go to St Joseph's at Takapuna.' Father Emilio rested his hand reassuringly on Papa's shoulder. 'The children will be well taken care of by the Sisters. And besides, it's only for a short time.' Papa managed a smile as he stood to leave. 'I'll inform the Sisters in charge at both convents that the children will be arriving on Sunday.'

After the rosary that night, Papa sat at the foot of the bed that we shared with our brother Etuati. 'You three are very lucky to be going to a convent to live. You'll have a lot of children to play with, and the Sisters will take very good care of you. You'll even learn to speak English like palagi children.' Our eyelids were heavy with fatigue. 'Father Emilio told me that you'll each have your own bed to sleep in.' Peka and I had always slept together in one bed. That's all we'd ever known. Papa's voice gradually faded into the black abyss as we slipped off into a deep sleep.

The bus ride from the terminal to Howick was long and bumpy.

'Why do we have to stay here, Papa?' I whispered, clutching Papa's hand tightly for fear he might leave us at the front door.

'Because we aren't allowed to stay together in the boarding house.' Papa's voice was impatient. It's not an easy thing to work and save up enough money for a home in this country.' He pressed his finger to his lips as he tapped on the front door.

'How do you do, I'm Mother Anthony. Do come in'. We followed the tall figure of Mother Anthony to the visitors' parlour where she and Papa talked for some time about our stay at the convent. 'While your daughters are here at Stella Maris, they will use their baptismal names, Mr Marks.'

'Yes, Mother.' Papa acceded without question.

'Now, who is Agnes, and who is Carmel?'

Papa placed his hand on my head first. 'This one's Carmel. She's almost four, and Agnes is six.'

'Welcome to Stella Maris, Agnes and Carmel!' Mother Anthony enunciated slowly, hoping we would understand.

Finally, it was time for Papa and Sala to leave. 'Va'ai fa'a lelei, si ou tei, Peka,' ('Take good care of your little sister, Peka,') Sala whispered. Peka's tiny head nodded obediently as the silent tears rolled down her cheeks. Papa and Sala then bent down, their stoic faces masking years of pain and struggle that they called 'life'. Gently, they breathed into themselves the life essence of my sister and me while pressing their noses and lips firmly against our cheeks. The click of the lock on the front door echoed Papa and Sala's hasty departure. Not a single word was uttered between them during the bumpy, two-hour bus journey back to Auckland.

Thick, hot tears continued to trickle silently down six-year-old Peka's drooping cheeks as she wrapped her tiny arms around me. With the palm of her hand she blocked out the piercing screams of pain from my parched lips. 'Don't cry, Lagi. I'm here.' Peka pressed her tiny lips to my forehead, to comfort me the way Sala did. She then wiped my nose clean with the hem of her dress just like Sala. It was time for us both to meet our new family.

Living together under one roof with Mama had become a living hell for Sala. Papa turned to the bottle and the company of other women to escape his mother's vicious tongue and her cruel treatment of his young wife. Once every fortnight, parents and family were allowed to visit us at Stella Maris. As regular as clockwork, Papa would don his grey pinstripe suit and catch the bus out to Howick to visit Peka and me on these Sundays. He always brought us a special treat of chocolates and lollies and sometimes even a tin of assorted biscuits. Sala rarely accompanied Papa on his fortnightly visits. Three, sometimes four, months would often pass by before Sala came with Papa to visit. Papa's excuse was always the same, 'Sala's busy looking after Mama and Mina.' Sunday morning was no different from any other morning for Sala. Swollen, broken and bruised, she would be standing over the wash-house sink, spitting out blood and sobbing alone, in pain.

Six months at Stella Maris saw the inevitable transformation of Peka and me from miniature Samoan immigrants who could not speak a word of English, much less understand anything that Mother Anthony, the Sisters or any of the children at the convent said to us when we first arrived, to fluent English-speaking little Kiwis — an achievement that Papa viewed with unadulterated pride. We ate our meals with a knife and fork. We wore pyjamas to bed. We rattled off the same Old English nursery rhymes and playground chants that our palagi Sisters were raised on. And out in the playground, Peka and I could belt out a Shirley Temple tune with the best of them. On Guy Fawkes Day, we all dressed up as a guy complete with sackcloth and blackened faces. On Easter Sunday, the Easter Bunny left baskets full of Easter eggs for everyone in the day room. On Christmas Eve, Santa Claus climbed down our chimney with a bag full of gifts for us all. And when our baby teeth fell out, the tooth fairy would stop by to collect them and leave a threepenny piece under the lucky pillow. Sala was now 'Mummy' and Papa 'Daddy' to Agnes and me, just like the other palagi children.

Our parents worked hard for two years to save the seventy-pounds deposit for our first home in Katherine Street, right in the heart of Freeman's Bay. The slums of Freeman's Bay were home also to other immigrants just like us, from Britain and Europe mainly, as well as Pākehā and Māori families from the country. They had come to Auckland with the same dream as Papa's, of a better future.

Every Friday evening after the pubs closed at six o'clock, Katherine Street vibrated to the coarse, crude sounds of inebriated workers swaggering towards their usual party haunts for their weekend's entertainment. Our father's afakasi relations and friends hustled their way to 13 Katherine Street where DB Bitter and Lion Red rekindled the pride that burned deep within them for the Samoa they'd left far behind. The Māori headed for Buster McMahon's house where strumming guitars accompanied the favourites from yesteryear that all New Zealanders, brown and white, loved to sing.

The familiar purr of the black Chevrolet signaled Daddy's arrival. Mother Anthony opened the front door and greeted Eti with her disarming smile. 'I expect life will return to normal for Agnes and Carmel, now that you have your own home. And I'm sure they'll both be a great help to their mother. The girls have learnt quite a lot during their stay at the convent.' Gently, Mother Anthony traced the sign of the cross on our foreheads for the last time. Our father shook the nun's hand firmly. 'God bless you all and may He keep you and your family safe and well in your future life here in New Zealand, Eti.'

'Thank you, Mother Anthony, for everything.' Eti bowed respectfully as the nun turned and closed the door behind her. Her work was done.

'Where's Mummy?' We had expected our mother to come for us today.

'Mummy's busy cooking a special Sunday lunch for us all,' our father replied in his best English. As the car drove off down the street, away from the cloistered walls of the convent, Agnes reached across and drew me close to her. The journey ahead promised to be long and bumpy.

Sui Not Su'e

Mua Strickson-Pua

Sui
is to represent.
Su'e
is to change.

Whakaatu
is to make representations.
Whakarere ke
is change.

Represent
representations
is to change
is change.

Sui
Su'e
Whakaatu
Whakarere ke.

SHE

Mua Strickson-Pua

SHE
works her hands
on the factory floor
sweat pours down her body
airtight suffocation
clock in clock out
spasmodic moments of freedom
wage packet goals of survival.

There
are children to feed
rent
to pay for a roof
electricity
switched on and off
her
church choir screams
family
fono on Friday
Aunty
Lisa's funeral
nephew
Amu's wedding
second
cousin Joe
faces court again

Ioane
wants a guarantor
Talosaga
beats his wife
drinks to escape the pain
children
come unstuck on glue
P does the rounds
Samoa
house project
back home calls
hire purchase on the car
rolls around again.

Samoa there
New Zealand here
SHE
is caught
in between
SHE!

Atuaology

Mua Strickson-Pua

Atua
Atua
God

Ora
ola
life

Whānautanga
fanauga
birth

Whenua
fanua
placenta

Karawheta
tauiviga
struggle

Tikanga
uiga
meaning

Matenga rawa
maliu
death

Tipuna
tupuga
ancestor

Haerenga
malaga
journey

Aroha
alofa
love

Rangimārie
filemu
peace

Bifobology

Christina Tuapola

What does it mean? Does this word even exist? It does for me, and eventually, I intend to have it inserted into the Oxford and Collins English dictionaries. It'll be one of my defining moments in history, and this is what I'll tell anyone who'll listen as to how I came up with the term.

So what is bifobology you ask? For me it's about the ability to translate messages at the speed of light, without making it look as though there was any work involved. It's about being taken off the island without removing your jandals and being able to infuse your footprints into the frozen winter roads in the city of Christchurch. It's about always being late for everything but forever having a wonderful and exciting excuse, which is accepted as true and correct. It's about the airport ground staff remembering your Island face, not as a first class Koru club member, but because you've missed every flight you've ever booked. It's a mix of all the above jellied together with a couple of cans of coconut cream (depending on which brand you use) and then marketed off as Island-fresh taro from the local Indian market – and reminder to self – don't forget to put it all on the account.

What is it about growing up in a proud community, whose fixation with family, church, rugby, food and fa'alavelave has inspired a foundation upon which a culture so rich has progressed into my own personal improvisation of bifobology? So let's just break down the word bi-fob-o-lo-gy into syllables and break down the explanation of my proposed definition.

My comprehension of biculturalism (and not the sexual undertones of bi) takes me back to circa 1970. Stand outside the back door of my family home and before you enter take your shoes off (too bad if your feet stink), come inside and do not speak if you're not an experienced linguist in the oratory of fa'a Samoa. Don't expect to leave until we've had lotu either. Most importantly, do not speak, unless spoken to, just smile (not too much cheesiness in that smile because it could be misconstrued as drugged smug). I forgot to mention, if my father doesn't speak to you, leave quickly and quietly and don't speak unless it's (you got it!) in Samoan.

If you were able to get into our home, sit upright, legs crossed in the sitting room (I didn't know what a lounge was until I was sixteen), and if my father walks in and looks briefly in your direction and gives you his infamous glare stare, followed by his reaction to switch off the light and shut the door, that is another clear indication that you should (you got it!) leave quickly and quietly. Two other important aspects of entering my home were: if you were female, you needed to don a traditional i'e lavalava (wrap around long length skirt) quick smart, and if you were male and your hair was at least 2 inches long, don't even think about knocking at the door. I learnt to become bi in the cultural sense and switch the signal in my brain off and on. It became an instinctive gesture that was natural and unfettered by my surroundings. Western society, it seemed, had to fit my parents' understanding of living in the cool and cold flora of the garden city.

This interpretation brings back a number of memories, all fluffy and poignant, some fanciful, some not, but certainly memorable. For example: 'Pring pack the bees, make sua or you poth wear it.' I remember the instructions, knowing full well that the actual translation was bring back the mixed veggies, or you'll be butt whipped regardless of how old you are. My brother, on the other hand, believing his mother meant beans was again to repeat an error in judgment. Whatever made him think 'beans'? However, I've always noticed my siblings (and I have many because

I was adopted) were not quick when it came to quiz games. I, on the other hand, was masterful to the point that it has triggered astronomical problems in my life for years. But that's another story, so back to the point.

I had so many broken-English instructions instilled in my memory that when a question was asked by one of my elders, I was a fast learner and knew I had one chance to get it right. The outcome was always: get it right and receive a new instruction. If it was an instruction with which you were familiar, reactions were good. However, get the initial instruction wrong, and a barrage of colorful language ensued, sometimes a slap, which I preferred. No matter what palagis try to tell you about that old adage, where the sticks and stones can break your bones crap, it just wasn't meant for people of Samoan heritage who are renowned for their masterful oratory.

As for the syllable 'fob', as far as I know, this has existed for me since the early 1980s and somehow channelled its way through the Samoan community like gossip on a grapevine, fast and intertwined in the New Zealand-born verbal mystique.

It's an acronym for 'fresh off the boat', except when I think about this term, for me it is a whimsical play on words because unlike my tangata whenua (people of the land – Māori) cuzzie bros' romanticised waka journey across the Pacific divide in the freezing bloody cold, my parents came to Aotearoa in the warmth and plaid of Air New Zealand styling. And, more importantly, they came at the invitation of the manuhiri (visitors to the land) government, with promises of milk, money, land, money, jobs and plenty more money. Fob is used loosely and often in our community, and I have even heard non-Samoans rattle the word off, be subjected to the stare glare and then run!

When I think about the 'o', my immediate thought is triggered by a vision of the *Wheel of Fortune* series. It's the most important series for all Samoans as our promising heavyweight boxer of the world was a contestant. The host asked my Samoan brother

David Tua for a letter, and the response was 'O, Steve, I like O for Orsome'. Or-some? O-righttttt ... You mean *awesome*! Never mind bro, just keep boxing!

As for the syllable 'lo', it can be attributed to a number of Samoan words or terms, however, I liken it to the shortened version of the word lotu, which means church or prayers. The word perhaps epitomises the foundation of our Samoan heritage and for some reason triggers 'Danger, Will Robinson, danger,' in my brain, purely because, although I was raised proud PICC (Pacific Island Congregational Church) all the way, the last time I entered church for a service was on my wedding day, and that was in December 1999. My faith in God is not fathomed by missing fellowship, but I feel my peace with God is emblazoned on my soul, especially since I can still recite biblical verses and hymns in Samoan and English at the drop of a hat.

I'm sure the danger signal is attributed to forced performances, where crying was not allowed as a child, for the wonderless event renowned to all Samoan children – White Sunday. It was the one day where all the Samoan children dressed in brand new white clothes (I always resembled a white Christmas tree, the only things missing were the fairy lights) tried to recite books from the bible in Samoan and English. The day would last forever, and it was followed by a toana'i banquet of food where kiddies fought over who sat at the head of the table.

It may not seem so bad, but we were made to practice at least three months prior to the event, after school until bedtime, all weekend from dusk till dawn. If you're not Samoan, and you're still thinking that's not so bad, well, add pinching and slapping to that practice and it's all good! My mother still claims to this day, she should've slapped me harder because maybe I'd still be going to church. I have even tried to use *The Da Vinci Code* for an excuse as to why I don't go to church. That didn't go down too well, and I was faced with having to explain myself to the church minister because my mother was ready to exhibit a performance that resembled a stroke.

The final syllable 'gy' has been added to make the whole word buyable for the public. If the truth be known, it is too difficult to come up with some wonderful anecdote to define 'gy', or for that matter, why would I create a breakdown of this syllable?

So then, after my translation of the word 'bifobology', weeded down to a few words for the final definition, I've come up with this:

bi – multi-talented
fob – fresh-faceted Samoan
o – with linguistic
lo – religious
gy – ties

Okay! So, my definition may need some work.

The Big, the Fat and Potato Salad

Aaron Taouma

Potato Salad

Aunty Lia loved her potato salad. She loved making it, showing it off and eating it too. This was her special dish, and at every family occasion we could always count on Aunty Lia's potato salad being there.

Aunty always boasted that she made the best Island salad ever, and because she used some secret ingredients, no one else's could ever compare to her wondrous and miraculous creations.

She was so proud. At every family do, she would place her potato salad at the centre of the main table and always made sure if there were other less worthy imitations nearby that they were pushed to the side or even sent back to the kitchen where she would be sure they would meet their deserved ends.

Aunty, and only Aunty, had the rights to the main table, and only she could do this because she was the matriarch of the kitchen and had the final say on what would be served, when and in what order. And, God help anybody who defied her.

This was all just a part of who and what Aunty was: big size, big pride and big ego. And, this was the way things were for as long as I could remember.

Things changed though when Uncle Sela died. This was a big funeral, and lots of our relatives came from all over the place: Samoa, the States, and even the ones who had been hiding from the family – some of them just around the corner.

The Stand Off

It all started when Aunty Lia and Aunty Iva were in the kitchen. Aunty Iva was from the States, and just like Aunty Lia, she was a matriarch of the family over there. She was just as big, just as proud and just as determined to have her fabulous creations sitting centre stage.

They had both brought potato salad and were arguing over whose was going to sit at the main table, whose was going out first and even over who was going to carry them. Aunty Lia wanted me to carry hers because I was the eldest daughter of Sela's brother. Aunty Iva wanted my cousin Moroni because he was her son and the eldest of our American cousins. Both Moroni and I just stood with blank faces, watching and waiting for some decision to be made and desperately trying not to openly display our opinion of how stupid our beloved elders were being.

To us the answer was simple, but, of course, we were only kids and so didn't have a say. And, before any answers could be given, Aunty Lia and Aunty Iva took the argument to another level. They got personal and they got competitive.

Aunty Lia started with why her potato salad was so much better than Aunty Iva's. Hers was made in perfect chunks, just like everyone liked it, with some spice and a special sauce that only she could make. On the other hand, Aunty Iva's was some mushed-up thing that looked like it had been through a blender and was as bland and tasteless as her and all of our American relatives for that matter – just a bunch of mushed-up American wannabes.

Aunty Iva retorted that Aunty Lia's salad looked like big bits of oil and fat mixed up with some food colouring to disguise just how disgusting it actually was. Then, she said that, yes, it was chunky alright, just like all of us New Zealand relatives – just chunky fob Islanders.

So there we were – one chunky and fattening, the other mushy and bland. They stood in opposition and glared at each other, resolved to their positions.

Walk Ten Paces and Turn

Now, it came to the competition. Both were indignant and the stand-off seemed to last forever. But, finally Aunty Nila spoke up. She suggested that the two leave it up to the guests, that we take both salads out at the same time and place them on the same centre table at an equal distance apart. Then, we could watch to see which salad was the most preferred.

Aunty Nila volunteered to act as a judge, and she pulled Moroni and me into it by saying we could keep a tally of the numbers that ate from each salad bowl, and we could even interview people as to which salad they thought was best. The two women stood and, hearing these words of wisdom, both agreed to the terms.

So it was, when the men and the guests came from the meeting upstairs to have supper, the contest began, and Aunty Lia and Aunty Iva both stood eagerly watching over the food area like hunters waiting for an animal to take their bait. They eyed everyone and could not help but try to edge them mentally towards their own salad bowls. This could be seen by the pained expressions on their faces, the raised eyebrows and the twitching of their eyes as they, not so subtly, tried to guide people to the bowl that housed their prized creations.

Quick Draw

As the night went on – it wasn't clear who started it, but when all was said and done, it was clear both were to blame – another argument started. Both women started verbally promoting their own product and even started physically guiding the patrons to it. And, when Aunty Iva asked the minister to have her potato salad, when he was clearly moving towards Aunty Lia's, that was it.

Aunty Lia exploded. She walked up to Aunty Iva and accused her of being a low-down dirty cheat. Then, when Aunty Iva ignored her, she went to Aunty Iva's bowl, grabbed a handful of her salad and threw it at her, saying that if her salad was so good, maybe she should wear it to show it off because that's what she was, just a show-off.

Everyone turned in shock, and Iva stood there for a moment looking down at her new nicely ironed Island dress now drenched in potato salad. She looked up, fire in her eyes, moved to Aunty Lia's bowl, grabbed a handful and threw it at Lia.

The two then went for it, and the food fight began. Everything was flying: chop suey, coleslaw and pisupo. It all ended though, when Lia picked up a bowl of oka and was about to plonk it right on Iva's head. Luckily, by this time everyone else had made it to the two and was pulling them apart. It was unfortunate, though, that this caused the bowl of oka to go flying out of Lia's hands and onto the minister's wife who had moved towards the fracas to see what was happening. And, this caused even more of a shock.

She stood almost in tears as another group of people rushed to her, and the aunties turned, looked and then started blaming each other for the accident.

'You big fat pig ...' 'You ugly ...' 'You no good ...' 'That's why your husband cheats on you ....' 'Yeah, well, I slept with yours ....' 'No, he wouldn't sleep with a pig like you ....'

It went on and on until finally they were dragged to two ends of the hall to cool off and get cleaned up.

Smoking Guns

This is when Uncle Faga came into the hall. He had been outside farewelling some of the guests when he heard what was happening. He came in and saw Aunty Nila seeing the minister and his wife out, and he saw the two aunties, now both crying to the two sets of ladies and onlookers that surrounded them.

He shouted, 'What the hell is going on here?'

And, there was silence, bowed heads and a look of shame on people's faces. Uncle Faga was the head of the family, and when he spoke everyone listened, and this was definitely one of those times.

He went around shouting and asking what had happened, and just as he was about to scold the two whom everyone was now pointing towards, just when he went to tell them, he turned and looked at everyone, and a sudden look of desperation overcame him. He quickly exited without another word, and everyone stood in puzzlement wondering what had just happened.

Then, it happened. It was faint at first, just a slight smell in the air, but then a rumbling sound from around the room could be heard, then strange looks on people's faces and movement towards the exit. It started here, but by no means was this the end.

People began clambering and pushing their way into the toilets, and Moroni and I and all of us cousins were having the laugh of our lives when we finally figured what was going on. That was until our cousins started feeling the effects too.

It was quite a sight to see, and the smell, well, the smell was unforgettable – just like the looks on people's faces and the groaning and rumbling, the twitching and hopping from side to side waiting for the relief that was to be found in the cubicles just behind the toilet doors. Some couldn't even wait for that, and some unfortunate accidents occurred as they were hurriedly trying to escape. It was truly disgusting as well as being hilariously funny. Everyone was sick, everyone except for our two aunties and me and Moroni. We were the only ones who were left to watch as everyone fell to the effects of the mysterious bug.

And, just when everything seemed to be as crazy as it could get, while everyone scampered around clutching their stomachs, all of a sudden, the sound of laughter could be heard coming from the direction of my aunties. In all the madness, somehow the two had found each other and now stood side by side as everyone else glared at them as the professed heads of the kitchen and those accountable for what had happened.

They stood and faced everyone together, and later when they had to explain themselves to the family in a special meeting held over the events of the day, they were united in their defence.

From that day until it was time for Aunty Iva to go back to America, the two aunties were inseparable. In the chaos they had found each other, and I guess the moral of the tale, from my point of view anyway, is that sometimes it takes a whole lot of shit before people realise the humour in their pettiness and can appreciate what they have in each other.

Pikorua

Janice Hy-bee Ikiua

3always and forever
Hawaiki nui is calling
To Te Papa Sun
Lanakila for victory
Keli for the strength in we
Near loss for Sunset beach
Forever-gained experience
Waka, vaka, va'a
All 'nesian ones
Journey 747 … final boarding call
Future brings it
Paying homage to past times
Dreams of culture moves to new times
Hula Halau of loving times
Ti leaves remember Pupukahi for all times
Never far from landscaped minds
Journeys of Hawaii ignited the souls

Mahalo nui

We love you so!

For the Love of Lia

Eric Smith

The stream at the end of Pause Road ran alongside our store. Sometimes it would reflect the sunlight causing it to shimmer like diamonds upon the back wall of the small wooden shop. From a distance the light would appear as if it were dancing upon the store counter, keeping tempo with the incessant trickling of the stream. It was something that always intrigued visitors, particularly those who had never been to our end of the street.

'From over there it looks like the light is dancing on your shop counter,' they would muse, gesturing towards the broad metal drive that lead to our storefront. From time to time children would gather there and delight at the optical illusion. The Pause Road Midday Matinee, I would think to myself, watching their realities suspended for a moment.

My weekday afternoons were spent minding the shop. It was a place that was ideal for me to complete my thesis and occasionally engage in conversation with customers and passers-by. When I think about it now, it accounted for such a huge slice of my life. More importantly, it would change everything, on a day that began with sunshine but was seen out with the rain.

The sun beat down relentlessly as I made my way home from school. I could see the store clearly. The pale blue paint, dry and cracked, still seemed so vibrant against the lush green palms that lined the retaining wall where we grew taro, banana and breadfruit. If you were lucky, a cool breeze would pass through, carrying with it notes from the pua (frangipani) that grew in thickets at the heart of the garden.

There was nothing extraordinary about today. I would take my place in the store, usually reading, till I closed at eight. I had just opened a book when I heard the subtle tapping of raindrops on the rusting tin roof. Slowly but surely the sky opened, and the tapping became an almighty roar that drowned out everything – even the trickling loop from the stream. Clouds gathered, covering the surrounds in a low key as the rain continued its thunderous applause.

On the street edge across from me, I could just make out a person running furiously towards the shelter of the storefront. I switched the light on in the shop, and as she drew closer, I noticed a satchel being held over her head in the futile hope of remaining dry.

'Lucky you were close to shelter when this came down,' I said.

'I don't believe in luck,' she replied.

She turned, laying the satchel on the counter, her fine slender hands pulling the long strands of dark hair back into a bun. She lifted her head, drawing a tortoiseshell comb from securely clenched teeth to hold everything secure in one fluid movement. Large eyes engaged me. I found myself looking into the most beautiful face I had ever seen.

'I don't believe I've seen you around here before. Are you visiting family?'

'I live over there.' She pointed at the rundown house situated directly opposite the shop.

'You must be mistaken. No-one has lived there in years.'

A frown rippled across her brow intimating disapproval to my reply. 'So you've never seen me before, and now you are calling me a liar?' She seemed quite firm, yet not at all angry. An apology was forthcoming nonetheless.

I fumbled. 'I'm sorry. I didn't mean …'

'Not exactly what I would call, you know, neighbourly,' came the reply.

Her gaze intensified, and in that moment, I felt something lift. Her grin almost prompted me to search myself, and sure enough, the recognition hit me almost as immediately as did the embarrassment.

'Is it you?'

'Yes. Did you think I had forgotten the promise I made?'

'Where have you been? Where did you go?' There were so many questions. The moment preoccupied me so that I had not realised the rain had become slow and steady, almost out of consideration for us who had, for so long, been apart.

'Promise you'll come and see me tonight.' She urged me.

'Where?'

Her head tilted to one side as she raised an eyebrow in disbelief, pointing at the house across the street.

'Of course. There's so much to talk about. There's so much I want to know.' And as quickly as the conversation had begun, it ended.

I watched as she disappeared into the shadows where the feeble glow of a lamp flickered from a window in the house across the street. The day had well and truly made way to the night, and my sense of it was fleeting. Everything had become about her – closing up at eight so I could talk to her and begin piecing the shattered memories and moments together.

Recollections began to fire, jolted free from forgotten recesses. I closed my eyes and drifted back. I found myself in that moment behind our house and beyond the garden.

I forgot her name. I told her to meet me in the cookhouse later that night. My skin was fresh from the shower, we only had cold water, and as I walked outside, I could just make out her silhouette in the moonlight and the way her ie sat high on her taut breasts and fell, only to break upon her young, shapely hips. I will never forget watching her as she stood waiting for me. I was unsure if she could see me as I was still in shadow beneath the fragrant moso'oi, but with each successive step, my heart beat a little harder as an immense feeling of joy washed over me. I could hear myself breathe.

The name kept eluding me, yet the picture grew vivid.

I smiled, plucking two small flowers from the pungent tree, placing one behind my ear. I was startled by a second voice. They embraced and kissed tenderly. I stood there frozen in that dreadful moment, wanting so much to react in anger. My fist unraveled, and the small, fragrant moso'oi fell to earth. They ran, laughing, into the garden.

I opened my eyes; it was seven to eight. I began to pack up and only then noticed the satchel on the counter. She had left it behind. I would take it to her. I straightened myself out, locking the store. With her satchel in hand, I made my way back out into the evening.

The night began to cool. The crisp air was refreshing and felt good as it worked its way into my ribs. The rain seemed less aggressive. Perhaps it had proved its point and wanted only to remind me that it was there. I picked up my pace so as not to become drenched by the time I crossed the road. I approached the house and waited beneath the far end of a bolster just beyond the reach of the lamplight.

There seemed to be a lot happening at the end of the house, which could not be seen from our shop. Several groups of people were dotted about, communing between the crush of vehicles parked haphazardly on the grassy verge. Nearby, two men were talking. They joked and then reflected solemnly as the sound of singing carried through the yard past the vehicles and into the bush.

'Do you have a light?' one of them said, gesturing with a striking motion as if holding an invisible box of matches.

The second man patted his pockets and produced a box, instinctively giving it a shake. He cupped his hands so as to preserve the naked flame, cradling it gingerly toward where the first man was standing. He managed to set the gas ring alight, sending the spent matchstick through the air where it landed at my feet.

'Have they finished?'

'Almost, but we best get started so as not to hold things up.'

I watched as they carried large pots from where they sat on a table to the cookhouse burners. Their forearms looked like granite in the flickering lamplight as they strained against the weight of the well-blackened boilers.

I moved closer, past the men in the cookhouse, past the pockets of whispered conversation to a spot near the front of her home. Where was she? Perhaps I should go inside and introduce myself. Through the broad doorway I saw people sitting quietly, listening to a voice that washed from the room that kept the light. I hoped she might see me and come outside. Positioned near the window across from where the lamp hung high, children sat at the bedside of an elderly woman. She appeared oblivious to her company or the numbers beyond the confines of the small room.

A middle-aged man with silver hair was talking. He was very distinguished. His address intimated that there were formalities taking place, an acknowledgment of some sort. He looked familiar. The tone in his voice was strong yet comforting.

'Thank you for your kind words and for your prayers.' The clarity in his speech suggested a great orator. 'Mum has been unwell for quite some time now, but she has given of herself to this family for so very long, with nothing but the interests of her beloved at heart. I will always be grateful to her for giving me the best of everything.' There were tears in his eyes, but his voice was unwavering. 'Every success in my life can be strongly attributed to the love of this woman.'

The old woman's gaze seemed to be fixed through the lamp on something beyond the room. The wrinkles upon her face rearranged themselves as she smiled at something or someone who wasn't there. I began to feel as if I was intruding. It was apparent that my visit here was wholly inappropriate, given what I had already witnessed.

I began to backtrack, hoping that I had not already raised the ire of the family, as would an uninvited stranger. I turned to leave, only to find her standing in front of me, smiling, as if she had stopped me short of not keeping a promise. She was right.

'Where were you going?' She questioned knowingly.

'I couldn't find you, and I wasn't sure if I should stick around,' I muttered. 'Your household obviously has some very pressing matters to attend to right now.'

'Which is why I made sure I got to you this time.'

I was caught short, not knowing what to say in return. She grabbed my arm and stood close to me.

'Well, I'm here now.'

The crying began in the room with the lamp. The sobbing swept through the house and crashed out into the yard. Figures scurried amidst the wave of grief that took hold of all who were gathered there. Her grip tightened as if to lend me some reassurance. The wailing around me became inaudible beneath the rain, which had again become very heavy. I turned to face her and was hit hard by an intense flash of light.

I flinched then instinctively looked up. Eventually, the glare resolved to form the buds of the moso'oi hanging above me. My head ached.

I could see the cookhouse that lay distant at the end of the garden. All I could hear was the rain falling upon the palms as the sound of laughter died away. At my feet, two freshly picked flowers jostled in a pool of water.

I lost her? The promise of her kiss or to hold her in my arms washed away with my tears, but the heartache held fast, defiant of the cleansing rain. I was heartbroken.

I made my way back through the thickets behind the cookhouse. The grass had become sodden. Before long, puddles of water turned into pools of mud. The moon held small concern and hid beyond the line of niu (coconut trees). The stars sparkled still, but tear-filled eyes caused them to flare like so many diamonds that blinded me. I lost my footing somewhere near the stream.

So this is it.

The rock beneath my head was warm, and the roof of my mouth tasted of metal. Unable to move, my sense of loss was complete. Inside was this hollowness, an unfathomable emptiness that would have easily swallowed the night. All I could see was the reflection of the stars as it danced across the rain-beaten stream.

The aching in my head had gone. The diamond reflections began to pale. As the downpour eased, my thoughts too began to clear. I could recite every prayer. I could recall every wish word for word. I could account for every breath and heartbeat that was the measure of the days I knew she was not here. The recollection of that fateful night had finally come home.

I whispered, 'Lia, I remember it all.'

Bus

Tim Page

John stood on the street corner feeling low. It was a cold, grey winter's morning, the bus was late, and he needed to go to the toilet. The bus shelter reflected his mood. Graffiti laden, broken windows, it neither looked attractive nor served its purpose of protecting travellers from the elements. Sharing in John's reverie were the usual crowd he gathered with each morning yet never made eye contact with, much less ever spoke to. There was the girl in the black woollen coat, with the obviously dyed red hair. There was the Samoan girl with tight curly hair and a face that looked as if it was designed to smile, yet was suppressed by daily circumstances. Then there was the middle-aged man in the two-seasons-back-from-fashionable suit, the battered brown leather briefcase and thinning grey hair. Daily they shared this experience, yet there was never so much as a word or even a nod of acknowledgement between them.

The bus finally arrived – the 306 to midtown. Silently the group arranged themselves into boarding order. Pneumatic doors swooshed open, and one by one they ascended the steps, inserted their smart cards into the reader and moved wordlessly to a seat. This early in the journey there were plenty of empty seats, so everyone followed the unwritten, unspoken protocol of sitting alone throughout the bus. So began John's day, just like every other weekday.

John stared out the window watching the suburban houses give way to apartments, in turn giving way to shops and office buildings as the journey progressed into the city. The bus took on more people, the empty seats filled up, and John found himself hoping that the person who would inevitably take the seat next to him would be slim, sweet smelling and without a large bag.

As John travelled this daily journey, he found himself reflecting philosophically on people, relationships and how the events of his past had brought him to this place. John was by nature shy and had always found meeting girls a daunting prospect. But he'd met Lynda through some mutual friends, and had immediately sensed a kindred spirit. After dating for seven and a half months, they realised they had something that could last. They were married fourteen months after they'd met and bought a small suburban bungalow six months after that.

For three years they commuted together to their respective jobs in the city – John in a bank and Lynda in an accounts office – in their eight-year-old Mazda. When they became the parents of baby Matthew, Lynda left her job to care for him full-time, and it was at this point that John commenced his daily bus journey so that Lynda could have the car.

The car journey, although a painfully slow plod through the city's congested traffic, had always been a pleasant time for John because Lynda was there. Together they would talk about the problems of the world in the way that only soulmates can. Now that John travelled alone with strangers, he missed Lynda's companionship and conversation.

Being the quiet, observant type, John couldn't help looking at his fellow travellers and wondering what the rest of their lives looked like. Where are they going? What do they do there? What do they do with their evenings? Their weekends? In the boredom of routine, John started making up stories about each of the familiar faces – their names, where they worked and what they liked. Then John looked past the passengers to the bus driver. The same driver guided their daily journey, but no one knew anything beyond what he looked like and what his job was. He was middle-aged, with classic Māori features and always wore his shirt sleeves rolled up to the forearms revealing rough, home made tattoos. Where does he live? What do the tattoos mean? What's his family like? How long has he been driving buses?

Out of all of these thoughts, the embryo of a plan was seeded in John's mind. The very next morning as John approached the bus stop, he deliberately looked for someone he could make eye contact with. The first person was the Samoan girl. She glanced at John as he approached, and he quickly smiled at her. Miraculously, she returned a slight smile. The rest of the daily bus ritual went as usual. But John smiled secretly to himself, hoping that he had started something. The next morning as John approached the bus stop, the Samoan girl glanced up, saw him and smiled. John replied in kind. When the bus arrived, John shuffled into the boarding line with everyone else, but when it came his turn to insert his smart card, he said a quick 'Morning' to the bus driver. The driver was a little surprised at the break in protocol but nodded and muttered a quick 'G'day'. John took his seat, but this time he sat nearer the front of the bus, and enjoyed his ride to work, strategising about his next move.

The next morning at the bus stop, John and the Samoan girl performed their now-established smile ritual, which earned a glance from the girl in the woollen coat. When the bus arrived, and the line started forming, John stood back and said to her, 'After you'. Her head jerked up in surprise at the breach of etiquette, but she managed to regain her composure enough to give a weak smile and a barely audible 'Ta'. The little band boarded the bus, and John repeated his 'Morning' to the driver. This time he was rewarded with a less surprised 'G'day, mate'. The bus lurched back into the flow of traffic. John sat in his seat and wondered if the lightened mood he sensed was real or merely his wishful thinking. The following morning when John arrived at the bus stop, something big happened. The Samoan girl smiled and offered a bright 'Morning'.

'Morning,' replied John. It was working! The man with the battered briefcase buried himself in the four-folded newspaper he always carried, but John could see out of the corner of his eye that the interchange had been noticed. There was no sign of the girl in the woollen coat, and John wondered what had happened to her as the bus rolled up. They performed their boarding ritual, including the newly established greeting protocols. The doors swooshed shut, and John was about to take his seat when he saw the girl in the woollen coat round the corner behind the bus, running awkwardly with her satchel. 'Hang on,' he called to the driver. 'Can you wait for one more please?'

The driver opened the doors, and the girl in the woollen coat staggered aboard, the hue of her face beginning to resemble her hair.

'Thanks,' she gasped to the driver as she inserted her smart card.

'Thank him,' said the driver with a grin as he nodded towards John.

'Thanks,' she said and smiled gratefully as she moved past John and slid into the seat immediately behind him.

The next morning when John arrived at the bus stop, the Samoan girl and the girl in the woollen coat were already there. They both smiled. The Samoan girl said, 'Morning'. The girl in the woollen coat said, 'Hi'. John replied to both. There was no sign yet of either the bus or the man with the battered briefcase. John felt a bit awkward. Now that they had greeted each other, there seemed to be a need to further the interaction, but no one seemed to know how.

'My name's John,' he blurted out.

'Hi, I'm Nina,' said the Samoan girl.

'I'm Samantha,' said the girl in the woollen coat.

After a few moments silence, the bus hadn't arrived, so John ventured another attempt. 'Where do you work?' he asked Nina.

'I'm a paralegal for Simpson, McPherson and Raines,' Nina replied.

'What about you, Samantha?' John prompted.

'I'm the assistant manager of a clothing boutique,' replied Samantha.

'Which one?' asked Nina.

'Cat Ballou in King St,' said Samantha.

'I *love* that shop,' said Nina. 'I go there all the time – wonder why I haven't seen you in there.'

During this interchange, the man with the battered briefcase arrived. There was a look of mild surprise on his face to find the usual silence of the bus stop broken by conversation amongst people who usually studiously ignored each other. He sat down in his usual place in the bus shelter with the broken windows and buried himself in his newspaper. John was wondering if they should ask him where he worked, when the bus pulled up, and everyone formed into a line. John deliberately held back to allow the others, including the man with the battered briefcase, to board ahead of him.

'Hi,' he said to the driver as he inserted his smart card.

'G'day, mate, how's it going?' said the driver with a grin. John noted that although Nina and Samantha had been chatting away at the bus stop, they still followed the unwritten, unspoken protocol of separate seats once they boarded the bus.

The next morning, John was at the bus stop, when Samantha arrived. 'Morning Samantha,' he greeted her.

'Hi John,' she replied. It was catching on! 'You didn't tell us where you work,' said Samantha, as the man with the battered brief case arrived.

'I work in the bank on High Street,' replied John.

As Nina rounded the corner and came to a stop by the less-than-adequate bus shelter, John and Samantha greeted her by name. Samantha smiled and responded warmly. The man with the battered briefcase looked distinctly uncomfortable with this blatant break in protocol. John noticed it, but Nina was oblivious to it as she turned to the man with the battered briefcase and said brightly,

'You're the only one we don't know – what's your name?' At this, the man with the battered briefcase looked visibly shaken.

'Umm, ah, Les,' he stammered.

'Where do you work, Les?' chimed in Samantha.

'Um, I work for the Department of Internal Affairs,' said Les, obviously unaccustomed to anyone taking an interest in his work.

John wondered to himself if this was the first conversation Les had ever had at the bus stop. At that point the bus arrived, they formed their line and boarded. This time, each one of them acknowledged the driver with a brief greeting. Each was rewarded with a smile and a 'G'day' from the driver, who seemed to enjoy the little interchanges immensely. John noticed that the driver didn't greet anyone else as the bus picked up more people on the journey.

The next morning saw another breakthrough. When John arrived at the bus stop, Nina and Samantha were already engaged in conversation. As John arrived, they both looked up, smiled brightly and greeted him. Les arrived a few minutes later with his four-folded newspaper under his arm as usual, but instead of sitting down in the shelter, this time he greeted the others and stayed standing as they talked about the thunderstorm that had swept through the night before.

When the bus arrived, they all boarded, performed their now familiar greeting ritual with the driver, but instead of dispersing to individual seats without any discussion, they all sat down together at the front of the bus where two seats faced backwards, providing four seats together. The conversation carried on, covering the burglaries that had plagued the neighbourhood in recent months. It turned out that Nina and Les had been burgled within days of each other and apparently by the same people. As the discussion and the journey progressed, John inwardly marvelled at how these strangers were slowly becoming a group of friends. From where he was sitting, John could also see that the driver was inclining his head slightly as if to listen to the conversation.

The next morning was the first time they ever heard the driver say anything other than a greeting. As soon as they started filing past the smart card reader, the driver blurted out to all four of them, 'How come you fellas know each other?'

'We all just met at the bus stop,' said Nina.

'It's weird, man,' said the driver. 'You're the only people who ever talk to each other on the bus, eh? I thought you must all work together or something.'

'Does anyone else ever talk to you?' asked John.

'Nah, I'm just the driver, eh?' he replied, with a slight grin.

'Well, tell us what your name is,' said Samantha, 'then you can be more than just the driver'.

'I'm Morrie,' replied the driver, 'and that's the first time any passenger's ever asked me my name since I been on the buses'.

A few of the other passengers were looking their way, obviously surprised at this turn of events. The bus stop friends followed the previous day's precedent, sitting down together in the seats near the front. Les started regaling them with an incident concerning his baby grandson. It turned out he could really spin a yarn, and before long, everyone was guffawing, including Morrie.

The next day when the bus arrived and the little group boarded, each one of them greeted Morrie by name. Morrie said 'G'day, mate,' to each of them, smiling broadly and obviously enjoying himself. When the bus stopped at a set of traffic lights that always took a long time to change, Morrie turned around and said to the foursome, 'I s'pose you fellas had better tell me what your names are, eh?'

The Risky Journey to Belong (Extract)

Florence Faumuina-Aiono

She saw him across the crowded room and, with anticipation, darted straight for him. She was so excited to see her friend Tony. He had been away on a family trip, and she couldn't wait to hear about his experience. Weaving through the crowd, she finally reached him and gave him a welcoming hug.

'Welcome home!' With eyes wide open with excitement, she begged him for information, 'So, how was it? Did you enjoy it?'

Solemnly, he said, 'I cannot believe that Samoa is so primitive. I hated every moment of it.'

Tony, a palagi, had just returned from a family gathering in Samoa with his new Samoan wife, Fale, and their infant children. He was a close friend, and as he relayed to her his disappointment of his first trip to Samoa, she became deflated by his experience. She knew Samoa would be a culture shock for him but didn't realise how negative it was going to be.

Naomi, a New Zealand-born Samoan, was already struggling with the fact that although she and her husband, Alec, were in their thirties they had never had a chance to visit their homeland – Samoa. They loved travelling, but Samoa had not appealed to them – for what ever reason.

This was an embarrassment to her as she had never been able to articulate to anyone where she belonged. She would describe herself as a Kiwi-born Samoan but had been challenged about that when she was told that the word 'Kiwi' correctly describes 'English

New Zealanders'. She didn't know how to speak her native tongue, and she never grew up in the culture. Naomi had to dream up her own belonging – her own culture. She still didn't know exactly what that was. It was a terrible burden to carry in a society that appeared to place her in different little boxes. 'No, you're not Kiwi – that's for English people.' 'No, you're not Samoan – you don't know the culture.' 'You look Samoan, but you try to be palagi. You're fiapalagi.' And so it goes on!

Trying not to sound defensive she said, 'Well, it's all political, you do realise that? Samoa is labelled a third world country – you know that don't you?' She was desperate to hold on to something and wanted to protect the Samoan pride. But, Tony was now speaking from experience, and she could not.

As she left Tony that day, she found herself pulled in all directions. She had expected it to be a culture shock for him, but she never imagined that it would be such a negative experience. It was difficult hearing that he had hated every moment of his trip with his young family. It was a devastating report about her homeland.

Up until that conversation, her husband and their two boys, twelve and five years old, were looking forward to experiencing a lovely holiday in Samoa in a month's time for the school holidays. It was the first time for all of them to visit Samoa.

So much preparation had gone into giving their children a wonderfully relaxed holiday with lots of sun, swimming, shopping, an easygoing lifestyle and touring. All attractions were booked and ready for them to enjoy. Naomi and Alec had put in some hard work to ensure that their first trip with their children was going to be an enjoyable one. They were all very excited. Up until now.

'How can I take my children to a place that cannot cater for their westernised lifestyle?' she thought to herself.

She felt selfish because of the self-seeking need for her and Alec to 'find themselves'. What a load of palaver! And worse was dragging their children into it. Naomi was confused and concerned for her children.

Alec was the calm one of the two of them. At least she could talk with him about how she was feeling, and he could say something that would help her rationalise her thinking.

'Hun, that's Tony's experience. We won't experience it the same way. Remember, Tony is palagi. He obviously wasn't fully prepared. We know what we are getting into; we are well prepared, and we know that we have done our best to put our children's best interests first by being practical about labelling ourselves as 'tourists' for our first trip. It's all going to be fine.'

That was somewhat comforting for her. If anything, it was going to be quality time with her family, and her children were desperately looking forward to that.

Everyone was up early in the morning. What a perfect autumn day to travel. The boys were excited and although Naomi was still internally anxious about the trip, she enjoyed the excitement of her children.

The flight to Samoa was smooth sailing. Very little to complain about. On time and comfortable. As 'spoilt' New Zealanders, Naomi and Alec decided to choose Air New Zealand as their preferred carrier – mainly, because they could not trust Polynesian Airlines. There was no logical reason for this except that they were westernised and patriotic to New Zealand rather than their home country! How bizarre is that?

Naomi was brought up in a single-parent home. Both her mother and father were from Samoa. Her father deserted their family when she was five. Was this why she had been anti about Samoan men? Or, was it because her mother always said, 'Never marry a Samoan man!' She took the chance and dated Alec in her twenties. Up till then she only dated palagi and Māori males. Alec was a close friend with great credentials, and her mother's saying did not connect with her in terms of this man. He was the very person who began breaking down the Samoan cultural roadblock that badly affected Naomi as she was growing up.

Naomi's mother didn't know much about the intimate details of the culture and never raised her children in it. Naomi didn't know anything about their heritage. In actual fact, they were brought up to dislike the culture and were proud of being New Zealanders rather than being labeled as Samoans. This was unusual for a Samoan family. It was apparent that without a father figure there was no cultural model to follow.

Alec, on the other hand, was from a family that held their Samoan cultural values highly. With a lineage of matai and a traditional aiga that used westernisation to their advantage without losing face of who they really were as Samoans. Naomi struggled with being brought into a Samoan family that valued its culture and knew its heritage. But because of Alec and his family's acceptance of her, she was nurtured into a beautiful Samoan family, began to learn about her Samoan roots and started a journey of belonging.

Although they were both Samoan, there was a cultural barrier in their relationship that, at times, would cause strong pulls. After the kids came along, there was clearly value-based cultural friction. Alec loved it that his children had their grandparents available to take them to Aoga Amata and traditional toona'i. Naomi wanted her children to go to normal kindergarten and to spend Sundays with her as a family unit, rather than the whole extended family that belonged to Alec. Naomi had no cousins to draw on, no aunties or uncles, so this was a mighty struggle. Could this trip thread them together in mutual understanding?

As the flight attendant checked to ensure seat belts were fastened, the family became increasingly excited. They were approaching Apia's runway and preparing to land on an island that they prematurely called their homeland. With eyes wide open and huge grins on all their faces, they anticipated a thrilling time. This was it. This is what they had all been waiting for – arriving in Samoa. It was time to settle the internal turmoil that kept them foreigners in New Zealand and alienated from Samoa. It was time to gain some experience to determine their belonging.

As they stepped off the aircraft they were hit by the heat, humidity and the beautiful palm trees that surrounded the runway. It reminded them of their trip to the beautiful island of

Hawai'i but the reason for them being in Samoa far outweighed joyful recollections of that holiday. Here, there was a sense of deep purpose.

As they entered the terminal, Naomi was quietly happy to see that things did not appear to be primitive at all. The customs officials were actually using computers. The interior was modern, and there appeared to be an order of doing things. She was very impressed.

It was 1.00 a.m., and their excitement grew as they moved up the queue and through customs. This was too good to be true. What was Tony talking about, Naomi thought to herself. Then, in a quick second, she was robbed of feeling content. Alec's luggage was missing. Alec spent some time going through documentation at the information counter, and Naomi and her two boys waited patiently. After an hour, the delay began to overwhelm her. Seeing her younger child sitting on his suitcase with hands carrying his little head at 2.00 a.m. was feeding her discouragement.

'What was I thinking bringing my children here?' she said to herself. Her heart sank as she comforted her little boy and as Alec stood at the information counter stressing his displeasure to the officials. Her oldest son began to visibly feel her concerns.

'Baby, it won't be long now,' she said with some guilt to her little one.

'That's Okay, Mummy, he said patiently and forgivingly.

She held him tight. She saw some Samoan men staring at her as she comforted her son, and she felt uneasy. She was an attractive woman. Their stares were making her feel very uncomfortable.

After an hour and a half they were ready to go through the security gates to whatever awaited them outside. But, for now, they wanted to get to their hotel, bathe and put their heads down to sleep in a comfortable bed, which they didn't need to make in the morning. Ahhh, that was a comforting thought that switched her into holiday mode.

As they walked towards the security gates, Alec was approached by one of the officials. She couldn't hear what was being said, but quickly, through Alec's body language and facial expressions, she could clearly see that this was not making her husband a happy man.

'I wish we were in Hawai'i,' she heard herself say. 'What's happened now?'

Alec cut the conversation short with the official and shook his head as he approached his family. 'Come on, Honey, let's get out of here,' he said, grabbing luggage and walking through the security gates.

'What happened, Honey?' she asked as she grabbed her younger child's hand and rushed up behind Alec for his protection from the line of officials watching them.

'They asked me to give them twenty tala for allowing us to walk through with our luggage. When I refused, and he realised that he couldn't get any money off me, he then asked if I was an Aiono from Fasito'o, and then proceeded to tell me that my aiga was waiting for me outside and that he knows our family very well. Total corruption, I'm not happy about this. They would rip off their own cousins.'

Naomi was in total despair but did not want to show her children.

As they entered the passenger clearway to unfamiliar territory and foreign faces, Alec recognised a face from a photo that his brother had given him. They began to feel safe as they were warmly welcomed, and their luggage was placed into a taxi van. The little visibility they had as they drove outside the boundaries of the airport gave Naomi and the children some calmness. Beautiful palm trees surrounded the area.

The drive through the villages stirred their interest. The roads were narrow and were not as developed as the ones back home. They expected that. As they settled into contentment and enjoyed the interesting journey towards the city to their hotel, they received some more mind-blowing news.

Alec's cousin apologised for a mishap in their hotel booking. They were not staying at the Tusitala tonight as expected. They were going to stay in a large mansion in Vailima that belongs to the general manager of Tusitala until the staff could find a resolution. This was the final blow.

The children began to ask questions. 'Mummy, what does that mean? Are we still able to swim tomorrow? Mummy, what's happening?'

As her temperature rose, Naomi cuddled her little one for comfort so that he would not be too alarmed, and she began to explode. 'I'm sorry, we are not here to spend any time in a house that has not got the amenities that my children need – I don't care how big it is. My children are here on a holiday, and we promised them a hotel with a swimming pool and not some house in a village. You need to sort this out quickly. I am not happy about this at all.'

Naomi always respected Alec's stance on things and always left confrontation of difficult situations to him, but her despair and guilt for her children in bringing them into this was too much of a burden to carry internally. Someone had to pay, and Alec was not interrupting. In his silence, he was giving her permission.

'I came here to experience my heritage and to find some belonging! I came here to give my children an experience of something that we have been robbed of for thirty-odd years – an identity! And my children deserve a swimming pool! You fix this problem, and you fix it fast!'

With that, Alec's cousin profusely apologised. Naomi's children clung on to her as a gesture of thanks for speaking up for them. By Alec's silence, her word was validated. She began to think about Tony's feedback. Was Tony right? Regretfully, she was beginning to understand and live his experience. Things had to turn around so that she could rescue this trip for herself, her husband and her children.

As they approached the village of Vailima they could see how beautiful the homes were. The mansions were cloaked with beautiful greenery and exotic flowers that they had never seen before.

There was nothing Naomi could do at 3.00 a.m. to change the reality that they would not be in their hotel room tonight. She couldn't bear keeping the kids up any longer and desperately wanted them to go to bed feeling safe and secure.

They arrived at the end of a driveway with huge, black cast iron gates. The driver hopped out and keyed in a code for the gates to open. 'Well, my house back in Whitby doesn't do that, so that's pretty impressive,' she quietly said to herself, eyes barely keeping open. It was a beautiful, huge house, but at 3.00 a.m., there was little that they could be impressed about. They were tired.

When they entered the house, they were shown their rooms, which were well prepared. They were in the bottom half of the house, which had its own amenities. The bedrooms were large, and as a precaution, Naomi decided that they should all stay in the master bedroom tonight. She wanted her family to be together for comfort and support after a rough start to their holiday.

The last thing her little boy said to her before she finally dropped off to sleep was, 'Mummy, am I going to be able to swim in a pool tomorrow? It's hot!'

The family woke up to crowing roosters the next morning. This excited the children. They were equally surprised when they looked out of the bedroom window and realised that there were roosters and chickens roaming in the backyard. They had never experienced this before.

As Naomi looked out the window, she couldn't believe how beautifully colourful the gardens were. The colours appeared to be richer and deeper than she was used to in New Zealand. Although, in her head, she was stressing over their accommodation, her soul was soothed by the exotic gardens.

'Mummy, are we going to our hotel today?' her older son asked.

That question took her back into the room, and she gathered her boys in her arms and said, 'I'm sure we will have a better day today.' Secretly, she began to lose hope and wondered whether the next two weeks were going to be disastrous. It wasn't that she wasn't grateful – because she was so grateful she had been able to sleep in a beautiful home last night – but rather it was not knowing what the holiday was about to bring. She had not anticipated any of the mishaps that had happened so far, in such a short time, at the beginning of their holiday. But, for now, she must not lose control in front of her children.

She began preparing the children for their day, asking them to jump in the shower and to dress. As they were getting ready, a messenger arrived, asking them to meet Alec's cousin for breakfast in the formal part of the house, upstairs.

The messenger also relayed to them that Alec's mother had called their relatives last night to make sure the family had arrived safely. Alec's mother was in tears and in total dismay when she heard that the family had had to stay in a village during the night. She didn't care what the conditions were – a village is no place for first timers like Alec and Naomi to stay in.

'This is their first time to Samoa. How can you let this happen? They are not used to Samoa's way of life. They are New Zealanders. Naomi and the children need to be looked after. You must get them to a hotel.' She pleaded to her relations. Her heart broke for Alec and Naomi as she was well aware of their New Zealand luxuries, and she desperately wanted them to enjoy their first visit to Samoa. Alec's mother was a well-respected Samoan woman who could put fear into anyone but in such a loving and humble way – you just did not want to upset her.

Once they were ready, they took the long staircase up to the next level. As they reached the top, it opened onto a modern home with panoramic views of the Pacific. A table on the veranda was set for breakfast so that they could enjoy the view.

'Wow, this is Samoa,' Naomi said to her husband as they looked down from the veranda into the village of Vailima. They had already been told the night before that Vailima was where the high-flyers lived. It certainly looked that way as they saw in daylight just how beautiful the island was. What a spectacular view.

As they sat down for breakfast, they met Beth, a middle-aged Samoan widow from San Bernadino, Los Angeles, who was renting the upstairs area of the mansion while visiting Samoa to begin her new freight forwarding business. She was linked to Alec's family and was a colourful personality, lively, carefree and a shrewd business woman.

As they had breakfast together, Alec and Naomi quickly relaxed as they heard stories from Beth about her love for Samoa and her business ventures. She had been living in Samoa now for three months, researching the way business is done in the Islands. She quickly realised that in Samoa it is who you know that matters. Alec and Naomi were fascinated. Lemeki, a Fijian man, came to join them and introduced himself. He was Beth's business partner and had travelled from Fiji three months ago to assist. He too sat down for breakfast and it was clear he shared Beth's passion for starting a business in Samoa.

Naomi, without trying to be snobbish, was quite surprised that a Fijian would chose to come to Samoa at all. Her ideas and perceptions about Pacific nations being together as one were a far cry from what she really believed. Although it was a bit of a struggle, it was a nice surprise to see that Pacific Islanders do work in unity.

The children had made their way to the front of the house and were laughing as they chased the chickens. Her mind rested as she heard them and so, without guilt, she continued to listen intently to Beth and Lemeki. Naomi could see that Alec was enjoying the conversation as well, as he too was an entrepreneur, in property. Prospects in Samoa could be rewarding for him.

It seemed that today was a good day. Perhaps, today things would turn around for them. The children were enjoying themselves in the front yard playing with the animals. Naomi and Alec were sitting on a veranda overlooking the Pacific, enjoying good coffee and good conversation. So, this is Samoa, she smiled to herself.

As late morning came, Alec's cousin turned up with some good news. The hotel had managed to confirm their two-week booking, and they were able to leave straightaway. Their room was ready.

The children became increasingly excited as they packed their bags and prepared to leave the mansion. A driver arrived for them as they thanked Beth and Lemeki for a beautiful breakfast and interesting conversation.

They travelled down towards Apia and saw things that they had only seen in colourful books at school. There were sights of villagers walking around barefoot and there were lots of smiling faces. There appeared to be a mix of modern and village living but a common theme of happy, colourful people.

There were old, noisy buses within the town of Apia. Naomi remembered the stories she had been told about these buses, and now she was seeing it with her own eyes. They were jam-packed with people sitting on the knees of others. She had heard that it didn't matter if you knew the person you were sitting on or not. The culture allows you to sit on others' laps regardless. She thought, 'You could never get away with that in New Zealand! You'd be arrested for indecent assault!' She laughed to herself.

They arrived at Hotel Kitano Tusitala. The pool had attracted them to staying at the hotel as their children loved swimming. The boys didn't waste any time. They children changed into their swimming togs and were gone! This was exactly what Naomi wanted for them – just to be free to enjoy their holiday.

Samoa was a beautiful place. Naomi could not help but think, 'This island is where my roots are. How blessed I am to belong. What treasures are there, waiting for me to find?'

Black Sheep

Douglas Poole

To Peter Ulberg-Stowers

I recall how grandmother would moan,
'Oi e, your Uncle Peter is the black sheep of our aiga,
He only sees me when he needs money or his girlfriends kick him
    out,
That boy makes me wild,' softening with alofa
'I wish that boy would come home, I miss him.'

Poy what a smile! Could light the darkness.
Those alofa-filled eyes, sowed a plantation of children.
Homecoming parties rocked the house!
Too drunk to pull each other up to dance to 'Born in the USA'
Laughing how Uncle Paul thought he was, aye!

Ioe, a child of the plantation; son of Gogo Sina.
            Old maps to the heart of the land, he knew best.
Took him from the aiga, only to return on a blue moon.

Ae, a child of Aotearoa:
            Found the old people who journeyed to Aotearoa,
In the Coromandel, of all places!

How the earth, the stones weep: Peter, why you never come
    home?

We are waiting. Rest your weary body in your father's fale.
Leave the sickness behind you, now you can sleep.
We will oil your body, dress you in your favorite kowpoy shirt.
Wrap you in the fine mat.

The whānau takes your body into the bush.
Far from your father's land, the title of so much contention.
Lay you here; you liked it best within the silence.
Gogo Sina will send another to replace you.
We await each other, to meet again in the children.

Blue Moon

Douglas Poole

Dedicated to Edwina Ulberg-Poole,
Vernon and Mary Mackenzie

Tuaoloa's garden nestles into the moonlight, a feast of breadfruit, mango, papaya, pineapples, yellow coconuts and sugar cane, behind the homestead of Henry and Tuaoloa Ulberg. In the homestead, the kerosene lamps have been extinguished, and the aiga are sleeping, all except Edwina, the youngest of five siblings – Uti, Fred, Maria, and Kathleen.

'Edwina,' her own voice tempts her. 'Edwina, come, we must go. Mary and Vernon are waiting.' She reaches for rolled-up clothes beneath her pillow. 'Climb out of the window, run, be brave girl. You are a woman now!'

Being titled and as employers of the aiga from Savai'i, the Ulberg aiga are considered noble. Maria always puts on airs and graces, telling her younger sister that a lady must never be seen without foundation, lipstick and earrings. This advice Edwina heeded, even after Maria left for New Zealand to work in Auckland.

Edwina's father has set the curfew for his children. Who would dare break the command of a matai?

Edwina and Fred once stole father's rooster and cooked it on an open fire up in the coconut plantation. Edwina stole father's horse and raced the Stowers boys along the beach. Yes, it is Edwina who has broken the law. She is in love. She climbs out of the window, runs down to a waiting car.

'Come on, Edwina, hurry up and get in,' calls her cousin Mary from the passenger door.

'Oi e, move over, Mary, you skinny bum!' Edwina giggles.

'Talofa, Edwina,' says Vernon, from behind the wheel of the coupe.

'How was your evening?' asks Mary.

'Father had a fono with the governor. Maria, Kathleen and I had to dance for him and his aiga. Oh, it was so boring.'

Vernon's coupe turns around, heads east, towards the back blocks. Mary and Edwina, in the back seat, fix their hair and apply make-up.

Edwina's father works in Apia township. Every morning Edwina sees him off with a kiss. Her spirit and beauty remind him of his mother, So'onofai. The aiga from Savai'i adore her too. She is the only afakasi Ulberg, who returns to Safune, Savai'i with her mother to see her grandfather. This is her heart. Tuaoloa blames the mischief on So'onofai, spoiling Edwina when she was a girl. 'Gogo Sina' was the title So'onofai gave her, and, like Sina, Edwina has a strong will.

'Oi e what is this!' Edwina winces on the hip flask.

'Some of my father's Scottish whisky' Vernon laughs, shaking his head.

'Edwina, will you dance with Henry tonight?' inquires Mary.

'Oh, I might. What about you, will you dance with the Yankees?' questions Edwina, winking to Mary.

'Oh, I might,' says Mary, winking back. They both giggle, knowing how jealous Vernon would be.

There is a story circulating amongst the young people, of a matai and a Yankee. The matai is a shape shifter. When he learns the Yankee is to meet with his daughter, he forges a vengeful plan. On the night, he possesses the form of his beautiful daughter and stands on a bridge overlooking the pale moon's reflection, waiting for the Yankee to come to him. The matai lures the unsuspecting Yankee into his arms. When he is about to kiss the beautiful maiden, the matai changes back into a man, gripping his arms around him, tight. The Yankee rips himself away, so terrified he falls into the water and drowns.

The open night sky shines; Edwina imagines the lights of Broadway, a boulevard of stars. She inhales the decadent fragrance of cigarette smoke and alcohol mixed with perfume – the heady aroma of contraband. Tonight she is not afraid of consequences.

The coupe pulls up and parks on the side of the dirt road. Her cousin Otto has organised the dance in a fale lit with kerosene lanterns up in the coconut plantation away from prying eyes or ears. A path of fire torches leads up from the road.

As they walk up the path, tall coconut palms sway in time with the ukulele. This could be a night in Hollywood or Havana. The young men wear suits and hats and stand together outside, smoking cigarettes.

The young women wear elegant dresses and stand together inside the fale, their beauty illuminating the shadows. On the dance floor couples touch and sway – the forbidden dance. What do they care for the shape shifter matai?

'Oh, Edwina, look, there is Aggie and the girls,' says Mary excited, pulling on her arm.

'Talofa, Edwina, you look beautiful tonight,' compliments Aggie.

'Fa'afetai, so do you, as always. How is your aiga?' asks Edwina.

'Oh, they are fine. We are establishing accommodation in town, for the Yankees. There are more arriving all the time. The war is moving into the Pacific.' There is a brief silence. 'Oh, look at us getting morbid, we are supposed to be dancing. Come on, let's go see all the girls,' says Aggie.

The young women stand together in a circle, sharing the latest gossip. They laugh and poke fun at each other. Laughter unites them.

Edwina glances over shoulder, pretends to go and get more umu or another drink. She cannot see Henry anywhere. Her heart sinks, though she is happy he is not on the dance floor. Then she hears a familiar voice from behind her.

'Talofa lava, Edwina,' welcomes Henry. He had caught her unaware, much to his delight.

Edwina turns to him. Henry's eyes quiver. 'Would you like to dance?' Henry asks.

'Yes, I would love to.'

Henry takes Edwina's hand and leads her to the dance floor. Henry gives the brows up to the trio of ukulele, guitar and vocal.

'Where have you been? I was looking everywhere,' says Edwina, her pride hurt.

Henry brings Edwina close to him. Her small body so fragile in his muscled arms, she is indeed a bird.

'I am so glad you came tonight, Edwina' Henry smiles.

'Don't sweet talk me, you know I had to sneak out.' She softens like cocoa butter in his hand.

'But I wanted to see you so much.'

'I'm sorry, Mina.' Henry moves his mouth close to her ear and whispers, 'I love you.'

Edwina holds Henry closer; in his arms she is free. She smiles remembering her grandmother. So'onofai told her never harbour worry, tomorrow may never come. Tonight she wants to siva. Tomorrow her father and mother may banish her to the aiga on Savai'i.

Brown Soul

Leilani Burgoyne

White skin.
White face.
White me …
Brown soul.

Where do I fit and how do I live?
Rip out my heart
… and show me its colour
Rip out my soul
… and locate my essence.

Nana, am I you?
Or are you me?
Brown skin, white skin.
Why?

Trapped in between
Constantly navigating
Always justifying
Me.

Voices that condemn
Judgement hounds
Categorising,
Classifying,
Trapped.

Are you really a Samoan?
You're not a *real* Samoan.
I thought you were a palagi
Ahh ... *you're an afakasi ...*

Wretched soul
Fighting, to justify.
Struggling, to be.
Brown soul trapped
Inside.

White.

Me.

Apia

Leilani Burgoyne

Sweeping reef,
Sleeping mountain …
Do you hear me whisper?

Under colonial skies
And vehement nationalism
Where
Are
You …

Tufuiopa,
Crumbling.
Aitu waters,
Papalagi bones,
Decaying.

I look for the space in between
Both Beyond and Within
Apia speak.
Show me …

… 'the beach'.

You

Leilani Burgoyne

I never really knew you.
And yet
I knew you best.

Round and Round we went
the racehorses,
the league players,
mcnuggets.
And again.
The racehorses …

Driving around Auckland
in your crusty-as car
A hole in your sock,
and an empty pocket
A heart full of dreams
and never a cent.

Always broke.
Always poor.
Always searching.
Always borrowing,
always singing,
always laughing
and always always …
talking

Passion bursting forth,
spittle everywhere.
Talk, Talk, Talk …
that's all you do
Your life blood,
your energy,
you …
Talk,
talk,
talk …

Bula Bula
you would say,
Malo e lelei,

Talofa Lava,
How did you know?
Why did you know?
Creator of Us …
Samoan Daughters,
Tongan Son,
Sons and Daughters …
Yours

Under the stands at
Carlaw.
Hanging out of
your car window
Falling out of
your car

Waiting
for you.
Shouting
at you.

Wanting
you back ...

A heart gone
Too soon
Burst forth
with passion
Explosion
of light,
Explosive
heart
Gone.

Pervasive
Silence ...
No more ...
Talking.
No more ...
You.

Palauli

Jason Greenwood

Anna Hahn was born on the island of Tutuila, American Samoa. Her father was a Swiss German who travelled the world in search of Eden. He found paradise in the arms of Teuila, a high-born young woman from the village of Leone.

Teuila was the taupou of Leone. Her grace and beauty were an inspiration to her people and admired by dignitaries and others who visited her village. She performed her ceremonial duties according to custom and traditions of Samoan culture.

Teuila died of complications after giving birth to Anna, and her Swiss German husband, unable to live without his beloved Teuila, died of a broken heart.

Anna was adopted by a wealthy half-caste couple from Apia, Western Samoa. Anna's grandparents decided that these people would provide their granddaughter with a palagi education that they could not give her, but when they returned to Western Samoa, they treated Anna as their servant, not as one of their own. Anna's early life was one of toil and sweat for these people who didn't love her. Her only happiness was the convent school she attended, where the nuns showed her kindness and respect. But the pain of many beatings and arduous work finally took its toll. Anna ran away. She went back to Tutuila, American Samoa. She returned to her village of Leone. Her grandparents had died, but the people of Leone welcomed her.

She inherited her mother, Teuila's, high-born status and carried out her taupou duties befitting her mother's reputation.

Four years later, two years before the turn of the twentieth century, Anna met Karl Schumann. He was a handsome German trader who had made Samoa his home. He courted Anna, showering her with gifts from the four corners of the world. Anna grew to love him deeply. Their wedding was a fusion of fa'a Samoa and polite palagi customs of colonial times.

Schumann bought a vast estate on the big island of Savai'i. Anna was to run the household while he established his plantation.

In carving out his estate, Schumann was ruthless in his treatment of his workers. Fear took precedence over respect and human dignity. He quickly earned the distrust and contempt of the people. Anna was unaware of her husband's treatment of his workers, but the whispers grew louder.

Schumann wanted sons after his own image. Anna gave birth to Paki, but her joy was shattered by her husband's total rejection of their son.

'This is not my son! He looks like a nigger, just like the rest of them.'

He accused Anna of being unfaithful. Schumann's outburst shook the foundation of their marriage – a marriage Anna thought was made in heaven. This was not the same man she married.

Two years later, Herman was born. Herman was fair and had the features of a Germanic prince. Schumann was overjoyed. He lavished all his love and attention on this blond, blue-eyed boy and ignored his older, darker son. Anna tried to redress the balance by giving Paki all her love, but the boy became deeply disturbed.

Herman grew to be at one with his environment; he loved to ride and fish. On his tenth birthday his father surprised him with a black stallion. A special bond grew between the boy and his horse; they became inseparable. The boy would gallop on the horse across the expanse of his father's estate and scour the coastline with fishing line in hand. On other days Herman would join the fishermen in their canoes or, in solitary moments, swim and dive in the pristine blue sea, his beloved stallion grazing patiently, waiting for his return.

In Herman's shadow, Paki watched and waited.

He was fifteen when it happened. The two brothers paddled their canoe through the channel in the reef and out into the ocean. The early dawn was tinged with anticipation. There were no clouds to mask the brightness of the day. The sun beat down mercilessly.

The screech of seagulls attempted to disguise the terrified sounds of a young man drowning.

'Paki! Paki! Save me!'

Paki's laughter chased the sea birds' cries to the horizon.

Anna's scream could be heard in the heart of the plantation. Herman's body was never found. Schumann's grief erupted; he turned on Paki. 'You killed him! You killed him! Du ungeheuer!'

'No, Papa. He dived into the deep and didn't come up.'

'You lie! You lie! Hermannnnn!'

Schumann grabbed Paki by the throat. Anna threw herself between them. Schumann shoved her aside. She hit her head against the post and lay unconscious at his feet.

The servants rushed to Anna's side as Schumann stormed out into the night.

Schumann's mood became erratic followed by long moments of dark depression. He would disappear into the night, return at dawn, then set off in the burning sun to drive his workers.

Anna found solace with entries in her diary. She wrote:

The edge of violence simmered in Schumann's presence. He drank heavily. One black, moonless night, he grabbed his rifle and shot the magnificent stallion. 'I want nothing to remind me of my son,' he raged. He glared at me while he said these words and barricaded himself inside the stable. 'I will kill anyone who comes near.'

On the morning, the day my husband died, I knew he was going to kill me when he returned. He had a look that made my blood run cold when he left the house to do his rounds of the plantation. When he didn't come back, I felt as if I already had died.

I felt my mother Teuila's presence that night, and when the thunder and lightening struck, he appeared in the room. 'Karl, Karl, why do you have blood running down your face?' He looked through me and sat in his chair by the window that looks out to the banyan tree. On moonlit nights its shadow entered our room. Our spirits live in the crevasses of the banyan tree, and their shadows also entered our room. The storm raged all night, and at daylight, I heard a commotion outside! Someone shouted his name. I looked at his chair, and he was gone. Oh, Paki! What have you done? Oh, Karl, I'm so sorry. Paki was only trying to protect me.

The people of Palauli said it was an accident. His horse fell and Schumann fractured his head on lava rock. The workers said it was an act of God.

Anna moved around the house in a daze for weeks. The terrified servants heard her talking to someone who wasn't there. They whispered that Schumann's spirit had entered her soul and was slowly taking possession of her.

Paki took over his father's estate. He sent for his mother's people from Leone to take her back. As long as she remains here, Schumann's spirit will inhabit her soul and damn Palauli for ever. He spat at the memory of his father.

Ominous clouds had gathered the evening Anna's people arrived to take her away. The servants had packed Anna's things with mounted fear. They believed the impending storm was Schumann's rage at Anna's departure. Her soul is his link to roam Palauli for ever. With Anna gone, he will be released to burn in hell for eternity.

Flashes of lightening illuminated the black sky, triggering explosions of thunder. Winds swept in from the ocean. The cyclone had arrived. The drama of light continued, striking the compound of the great house. Terrified, neighing horses, bolted into the chaos beyond. The stable where Paki had fled was a mass of flying timber and corrugated iron – a once solid structure, now stripped in the grip of destruction. Paki was heard screaming in the eye of the storm. 'I defy you father! I defy you!'

Palauli lay in ruins. Only the banyan tree stood, defiant.

Paki's body was found at the bottom of the channel, amongst debris dragged in by the violence of the storm. Beside him lay the bones of a boy who once rode his stallion and played in the sparkling waters that danced beyond the reef.

Anna emerged from the banyan tree. She was protected in the home of the spirits. She re-established her husband's plantation.

She built a fale on the headland overlooking the reef. There she would sit, reliving her past. Two graves lay in sight of the fale, the headstone facing the channel in the reef. The inscription read: In loving memory of Paki and Herman Schumann, beloved sons of Karl and Anna Schumann. Rest in peace.

A soft breeze kissed Anna's cheek. She looked up and smiled. Thank you, Karl. Palauli is restored, once more.

No Sex Please, We're Disabled

Chris Baker

Michael and I were laughing in the corridor the other day. He'd been watching *Oprah* when they were discussing the plight of a woman who'd enjoyed only one passionate interlude in four years. I didn't know Trudy was standing right behind me when I opined to Michael that it was probably better to have one good bonk every four years than an indifferent one every night. Michael chuckled and from behind me came a burst of laughter, which is when I realised Trudy was there.

Sex is really a no-go area here in the Leslie Groves Hospital. I mean, here are us residents, wheelchair-bound and utterly dependent on the nurses for the most intimate functions like bowel motions and catheter changes, lying back and thinking of the queen while we get put to bed, got up, showered, dressed and undressed. And it's surprisingly easy. It's like I said to Michael's twenty-eight-year-old daughter who was visiting and happened to overhear somebody in the dining room discussing their bowel motions with the sort of casual yet intense interest that usually characterises conversations about politics or gardening.

'It's different in here,' I said, all avuncular to this young woman wearing a T-shirt that proclaimed in 10-centimetre letters, 'PSYCHO BITCH'. 'In the outside world, people's obsessions revolve around sex and death. In here, they're concerned mainly with incoming and outgoing.'

But if the truth be known, we're very much concerned with both sex and death, even if sex is very like Chekhov's white bear.

When he was a boy, Chekhov formed the White Bear Club, membership of which was gained by standing in a corner for half an hour and not thinking of a white bear. Try it. Prepare to be amazed at the proportions that a white bear assumes. It's like that with sex. Your condition and a few other factors like crappy diet and lack of exercise leave you soft and pudgy, with all the sexual allure of a sea cucumber. But that doesn't stop you thinking about sex, maybe even living in hope. I'm certain some of us like to imagine we're still God's gift. I sure as hell don't. My years as a journalist left me with a bullshit detector I couldn't turn off even if I wanted to, and everything I think and feel comes under its merciless scrutiny.

So I'm left making jokes about sex, and even there, I'm picking my way through a minefield. But I'm usually safe with Viagra jokes. I come across a few of them, often via Alex who moves in some interesting circles. She's one of life's genuine aristocrats, more class than most people can handle, but she'd be at home walking any street I've ever been on. She produced the one about the Viagra eye drops – poke 'em in your eye and take a good hard look at yourself. And I heard a ripper from Frank, via Linda, his wife. They're both Geordies – check out *Auf Wiedersehn, Pet* – they're off later this month, and we'll miss them both when they go.

Anyway, Frank had a stiff neck the past couple of days, and Michael was teasing Linda about how he might have acquired this.

'No, no,' I heard her say. 'What happened was he was taking some Viagra, and a pill got stuck in his throat.'

Most of the nurses here have that sort of earthy attitude, except for one or two who are perhaps a little naïve. There's one woman who's very big on keeping 'laura norder'.

'If you don't eat all your veggies, I'll smack you,' she keeps saying to me. Every time I'm tempted to ask her if she plans to wear her nurse's uniform during the disciplinary procedure or does she have in mind some cheeky little leather number. So far, I've managed to button it in time, but I'm worried she'll catch me in a caustic mood, for instance, when the latest culinary offering from Ace Foods would probably qualify as a weapon of mass destruction.

This same woman often comes into my room looking for somebody.

'Are you hiding a nurse under your bed?' she asks. Indeed I am not, I reply. Why on earth would I keep a nurse *under* my bed? It would make far more sense to have the nurse *in* the bed, were I ever unhinged enough to harbour such a fantasy.

My urethral catheter was a sure-fire deflator of the libido. Frank told me about a hospital in the UK that produced pamphlets showing how sex with such a catheter is possible. The mind boggles. I haven't yet met a woman who'd be lifted to higher plateaux of passion by the involvement, in whatever the erotic activity might be, of a foot of plastic plumbing. I remember very clearly the day John Boleyn, the chief nurse who manages this place, was demonstrating on me to Ann, the registered nurse who runs our ward, how to remove an old catheter and insert a new one. John, a two-metre Dutchman built like an All Black prop, doesn't lift my skirts by the merest fraction. He fixed his gaze upon me and spoke grimly.

'This procedure has no erotic content,' he pronounced, while poking a catheter up my willy. I almost laughed. I've been involved with few activities that had less erotic content; in fact, the whole business failed utterly to bring to my mind even one or two of the nine billion names of God.

It probably helps you to survive in this vale of tears generally, and here in particular, to have a good awareness of your own sexuality. In fact, if you're disabled you'll need that awareness, especially in the interests of surviving society's prevalent attitude towards disability, for which you can probably substitute the word 'disqualification'. In other words, how dare you view yourself as a sexual being? You're less than physically perfect, and the thought of you in the throes of passion is utterly distasteful to any 'normal' person. Well, sorry to disappoint you. I've long been aware that my most powerful sexual organ is located between my ears, and the women I find most attractive have a similar awareness. And none of them give me any signals, except for Alex, but that's none of your beeswax. And naturally, none of the nurses here gives off any signals, which is fine by me. Displays of body parts won't do it and nor will dirty talk and not the proximity of women either. Don't get me wrong. I'm probably in love with most of the women on the planet, especially Macy Gray who has size ten feet, but I enjoy my sexuality, and I guard it very carefully.

A Requiem for a Dream

Marisa Maepu

When the dreams first started, I didn't recognise the great writer. He appeared as a blurry figure, and when he tried to speak, the sound was muffled and eerie. A black hole featured where a mouth should have been and two red smudges were eyes.

I woke up in a cold sweat after that first dream. I was shaken, and my senses had switched to high alert. As I lay there, I thought I could hear screaming, but when I listened harder, there was nothing. My eyes played tricks on me too. I saw moving shadows in the room, interspersed with flashes of vivid white lights. I'm going mad I thought. I pressed myself closer to David's warm sleeping body, trying to calm myself. What had I done to befall the misfortune of being visited by an aitu?

The dreams continued. It became apparent that it was indeed an aitu who was frequenting my dreams, but the aitu was friendly, thank God. With each passing dream, his features slowly came into focus. A gaunt face, a tall, thin body, a prim Scottish moustache. Finally, the unmistakable figure of Robert Louis Stevenson materialised. My fear instantly subsided when I realised who the aitu was. An intense excitement washed over me then.

I knew very little about the remarkable Robert Louis Stevenson. I knew what an esteemed place he held in Samoan history as the tusitala, and it made me feel special. I even felt an element of invincibility, as though my communication with him somehow made me more akin to them – the dead – and, by association, I was not of this world either.

★★★★★★

This morning, I tell David about my dreams and how excited I am about them. David gives a deep and tired sigh behind the newspaper he is reading. 'Dreaming of another man? Excited, huh? And do you do *it* in these dreams?'

I ignore David's patronising tone and laugh uneasily. 'They're not those kind of dreams.'

David finishes his coffee and goes to work, leaving me feeling alone and silly.

★★★★★★

The dreams are becoming more thrilling. Robert speaks to me in a Samoan form that I believe is old-Samoan speak, maybe like that which was spoken in his time. It is a metaphorical and lyrical Samoan I have never heard before, in my dreams or elsewhere.

We talk for hours, Robert and I, in my dreams. I sense he is lonely. He must have known I was kind of lonely too. He talks of Scotland and of Samoa. *His* Samoa. I tell him about Samoa and about Samoans of today. I tell him of Samoa's move to national independence in 1962 (and he was overjoyed). I tell him that, despite independence, the effects of colonialism continue to hinder many Samoans.

I describe to him the new developments that humankind has made, the breakthroughs in science and technology and travel around the earth and into the realms of space. He marvelled.

I also tell him about wars, disasters, poverty, terrorism, new diseases and the destruction of the earth's resources. He is philosophical about this. Jekyll and Hyde, he says, and he tells me about the necessary balance of good and evil in men.

We talk for hours in my dreams, and I am always eloquent and charming and knowledgeable. Robert is a patient listener and a thoughtful friend. He is often too sick to talk, and sometimes his image would fade away. I figured that when this happened it was the tuberculosis taking hold – the unforgiving illness that gripped him as a little boy and never let go.

★★★★★★

Tonight, Robert and I sit on the sea wall on Beach Road in Apia. It's dusk, and the sky is quickly darkening.

I ask him, 'Why do you visit me?'

'I have some regrets in my life, and I need to share them with you.' He is frank, and I let him talk.

'I regret that I never had children of my own to carry on my name and legacy. I regret that I didn't tell Fanny more how much I appreciated her. I regret that this wretched sickness overpowered me too soon.' He stopped, and as if on cue, a coughing bout overcame him. His image flickered violently, as if he was going to disappear, but then he recovered. 'But my biggest regret of all, the thing that brings my spirit to visit you, is that I left this world before I could complete my best work.' He looks sad, so I touch his arm, and my fingers go right through him.

'But, Robert, you gave so much to the world – *Treasure Island*, *Kidnapped*, *Dr Jekyll and Mr Hyde*, *A Child's Garden of Verses*, *Island Nights Entertainments*.' In my dreams, I knew all his writings.

He shakes his head. 'Yes, but I was writing my ultimate work when I died. I thought I had more time ….'

'What was it called?' I ask with uncertainty, but he replies freely.

'*The Weir of Hermiston*'.

We are quiet again for a long time, Robert and I, in the dream space of neither here nor there. He asks me then whether I would finish his story for him. He asks whether he could tell me the rest of the story and I could write it down and share it with the world. When I turn to respond to him, he has gone. I look around and find that I am no longer sitting on the sea wall in Apia; instead, I am in the house I lived in as a child.

★★★★★★

I try to carry on as normal. I go to work. I try to care about what is going on at work, about business and customers, but the feeling is false. I don't care at all. I cook dinner in the evenings, and David and I eat in silence in front of the television. I had stopped telling David about the dreams, and because the dreams are all I think or care about, we hardly ever talk.

As I have for the past two years, I phone my mum and sister in Auckland on Sunday night. I muster up the courage to tell my sister about the dreams. I feel relieved to be finally sharing my experience with someone, and as I talk, I find myself growing increasingly excited, especially when I tell her that Robert planned to tell me his unfinished story very soon. Sina listens quietly as I explain. I tell her everything, and when I finish, she laughs like a wild monkey. She laughs her loudest meanest laugh – the one I hate when directed at me. I withdraw into myself then. If Sina didn't believe me, then there was no hope that anyone else would.

★★★★★★

I'm like a streetwalker or vampire; I live for the night now. The day and the waking hours are just void time, waiting time, until I can go to sleep and re-enter the blissful world of dream.

My nightly routine has become a considered process. I go to bed at least two hours before David (he is on my list of banned stimuli, which also includes TV and radio). I arrange pen and paper on my bed stand, prepared to write down precious recollections of my dreams. I make sure the room is the right temperature, and I always have a glass of water nearby, in case dehydration adversely affects my slumber.

★★★★★★

The phone rings while I'm with a customer. I'm surprised to find out it's David. 'What's up, David?'

'I thought, ah, maybe we could go out to dinner tonight.' He sounds nervous.

'What's the occasion?'

'Well, because it's Valentines Day, and that's what couples do. Besides, we haven't gone out for a long time. I think we need to get out of the house and do something fun. We need to talk too. We really need to talk. Things are different ….'

I panic. I was planning to go to the library tonight. I wanted to get some of Robert's books and read before bed. I had already read a few in secret, biographies on him too.

I couldn't tell my plans to David. I knew how crazy it would sound. Robert Louis Stevenson was visiting me every night in my dreams, and wanted me … *me* … to finish his greatest ever untold story. It sounded ridiculous – even to myself. David would laugh if he knew. Besides, David was the clever one. He was well read and well educated. Not me. And if for some bizarre reason it was true that Robert Louis Stevenson was communicating beyond the grave, then why would he pick me for this great honour? Surely there were more deserving people.

I make up an excuse. 'I'm not really feeling that great actually. I'd rather just have a quiet one at home. Sorry.'

I think David is disappointed, but I'm not sure. I consider going for a run after work. I always sleep better after exercise.

★★★★★★

I'm in the dream space. I know this, because I feel a lovely mixture of calm and glee. I am different when I am here. I'm a better version of myself. David doesn't know the me of these dreams, the clever and witty and beautiful (always beautiful) me. I see Robert approaching. My heart soars.

★★★★★★

One night after a run, David asks me whether I'm having an affair. I stop in the hall, sweaty and breathless.

'What?'

'Why the sudden interest in looking after your body?' he goads.

'I just want to sleep better. The exercise helps,' I reply.

'You seem to sleep fine to me,' he says.

The accusation enrages me, but I bite my tongue and head quickly for the shower.

★★★★★★

The dreams have become less frequent, and this has caused me no end of anxiety. I decide that David's negative energy has affected my sleeping patterns and my dreams. It makes me resentful. I think of asking David to move to the spare room.

★★★★★★

Finally it happens. Robert visits again, and I sense this is the big night. We are in a Victorian-styled room. He sits in a rocking chair, and I sit facing him on a large bed. The room is very warm as there's a healthy fire burning in a huge fireplace. I guess we are in his Vailima home. 'Where's Fanny?' I ask, feeling suddenly awkward and guilty.

Perhaps Robert doesn't hear me. He has a faraway look on his face when he says 'Are you ready? I'll now tell you the rest of *The Weir of Hermiston*.'

I'm immediately mesmerised. A notebook and fountain pen appear on my lap, so I write and write in a frenzy while Robert narrates. The story is perfect. When at last he finishes, he looks at me and is suddenly vulnerable. He asks whether I like it.

'Yes, Robert, of course,' I gush. 'It was amazing, Robert. Thank you.'

'Ana!' A distant voice is calling me. Suddenly the voice is deafening as if right in my ear.

'Wake up! Ana, wake up!'

'Huh?' I'm groggy, in the murky and warm space of dreaming.

'Ana! You're sleep talking! Wake up! You're sleep talking.' David is looking down at me, his eyes accusing. 'Who's Robert?'

I pull a pillow over my face, not wanting to be awake.

'Who's Robert?' David is yelling now. 'Who's Robert?'

I sit up to face his rage, and I feel suddenly scared. I struggle to think straight. My words are frantic now.

'Remember those, um, dreams I was having about … ah … about … Robert Louis Stevenson? It's him. It's just him. It's just dreams ….'

He glares at me with disgust. 'Is that the best you can do? Can't you give me a better excuse than that? Do you think I am that stupid? I know you are hiding things from me. You don't tell me where you're going. You don't talk to me any more. Don't lie to me any more.'

His words are a swift slap in the face. In the back of my mind, I think what he says is true. I can't answer him.

'It doesn't matter any more,' he says, getting up, and pulling on jeans and a T-shirt. 'It doesn't matter any more. I've had enough.'

He leaves, and I lie there for a while staring at the ceiling. I try to go back to sleep, to the dream place where I feel happiest, but for the rest of the night, sleep evades me.

The next day I have only a vague memory of the dream. I try desperately to remember details. I know the dream was important, but I can't remember why. I remember a notebook and search for it. Then realise that I had only dreamed it. It's not real.

David calls later that morning to say he is staying with his brother and will come that evening to get his belongings. He's moving out. I cry a deep cry of utter despair. I feel ashamed because I don't know whether I'm crying for David or because I can't remember my dream.

★★★★★★

I never dream again after that night. David left me and somehow took my dream ability with him. I block everything out. My future means nothing to me now. Life is empty. Bleak. Dreary.

I see David around now sometimes, at the supermarket or on the street. We pretend not to see each other. He looks a lot older now. Haggard. He's lost weight, and his tall frame looks fragile. He has grown a moustache too. Funny, he reminds me of someone I used to know.

The Dancers

Sia Figiel

There is a river in the middle of a flower. And in the river there is a blue bird. And the blue bird is singing a song. And in the song is the story of a woman with red hair. And the woman is not singing, but her lips are moving, and her eyes are closed, and she is looking into the dark that clouds her dreams. And in her dreams there is a man, tall and handsome in a military uniform. And the man is smiling. There is a snake crawling on his arm. The snake is wrapped around a naked woman. Not the woman who dreams but another woman entirely. This woman with the snake around her naked body has a grin like the *Mona Lisa* on her green lips. That's what the tattoo on the man's arm looks like.

1959. A ship arrives in the Pacific Island of Love. The ship is greeted by a dance group from the village of Obligation. Boys and girls and men and women and old men and old women greet the sailors with arms extended, each with an ula or a necklace of flowers to present to the visitors. The sailors are in blue. They are smiling at the children. They are smiling at the men and women. They are smiling. The children think they're the friendliest human beings to ever walk their island.

Among the dancers is the woman with red hair. She is dancing silently. And in her silence there is a deep ocean. And in the ocean there is a post office. And in the post office there is a man in a locked room. He is wearing formal attire and looks important. That is, he is wearing an iefaikaga and a perfectly ironed white shirt and tie. There are degrees on his wall with his name on them. He is a certified accountant. He is a certified translator. He has a Bachelor of Arts in English as well. Below the degrees is a photograph of himself and three children. The photograph is in black and white.

The man in the post office is smoking a cigarette. Lucky Strikes. There is a line of men and women outside the post office. They wait with flies on their legs. The man takes a puff. And another and another. His mind travels to the color red. And as his mind travels, he remembers meeting the woman the night before. He remembers each word he whispered in the wind in her ear, and it pains him to know that the woman does not think of him the way he thinks of her.

My heart dies each time I see the colour red
My heart dies each time I see the colour
My heart dies each time I see
My heart dies each time
My heart dies
My heart

It is raining in the dream. The raindrops are falling on the petals of the flower. Falling on the water that is the river. The leaves of the river bank trees shiver. The woman runs into the river. Soaks her suffering in the cold of the river. Does not shiver from the cold. Is instead comforted by it. She emerges from the cold of the river and begins running up a mountain. Her legs bleed. Her feet bleed. The woman runs and runs still.

They meet again. This time in the day. She is buying a stamp at the post office. She is wearing a floral cotton dress. Her hair is perfectly combed and pinned in a bun. She wears red lipstick. Red shoes. Red earrings and a watch with a red leather band. Her entire outfit matches the red bag she carries. The red bag is made of bamboo. And in the red bag there is a letter. She lifts the letter out of the bag and gives it to the clerk. The clerk demands ten sene for the postage. The coconut sways behind the ten sene mark in the stamp.

I don't know what you're asking me, Blue
I don't know what you're asking me
I don't know what
I don't know
I don't

They are in the office. The office with degrees on the wall.
The man tells the woman to remove the pins from her hair. He
also tells her to wipe the lipstick from her lips. The woman says
nothing. She tells the man that she is on a break and that she needs
to get back to the studio. The man says the studio can wait. They
have you the rest of the day, and I only have you for an hour. Isn't
that enough? No. Never.

There is a knock on the door. A woman's voice accompanies
the knock. There is a telephone call for you, Sir. It's your wife, Sir.
But he does not hear the call. His head is lost. Lost in the woman.
Lost under the woman's skirt. So that if someone were to walk
into the office, they would only see the woman sitting at the chair
facing the degrees. They would not be able to see Sir because he
would not be seen from any direction. He is under the woman's
skirt, and she, the woman, appears to be dancing a slow dance in
the chair in which she is seated. A slow, slow, slow dance. One she
would never perform in a public space. Reserved only for a locked
room in the middle of the post office.

The dance is a dance that women from Obligation village
were banned from performing since the arrival of missionaries
almost 150 years before. Whenever a man would ask a woman if
she wished to dance this dance, a woman of virtue would deny
outright even having knowledge of it. I don't know what you're
asking me, Blue, is how the woman replied to Sir's request to
dance. Her mother is the head of the women's committee. Her
mother is the head of many organisations within the village. She
is known in the village and throughout the district as a tyrant.
Several men have come to the house to ask for her daughter's hand
in marriage. She has refused them all. They were not worthy. Not
worthy. Not worthy. Not.

She is twenty-seven. He is forty-eight. He is a professional dancer. He knew that at her age she did not know how to dance this particular dance. He was convinced that she had never in fact danced it before. A dance he had danced ever so often with women, particularly palagi. It began when he had asked the wife of a diplomat to dance once. He was attending a function at the High Commissioner's house up at Vailima. He was alone. He always attended these functions alone. That is, without his wife. The guests were gathered in the living room, and they were talking about a particular objet d'art the diplomat had presented his wife upon his return from a meeting in Bangkok. It was an eighteenth-century canopy bed, which used to belong to the son of one of the ancient kings. And while the guests were examining the bed and its illustrious design and exotic beddings of silver and gold, Sir slid out to take a puff of his Lucky Strike. As he was about to light the fag, a pale hand lifted a lighter towards his face. He looked at the fire and saw the moon that shone behind it. For that was the color of this woman's face, which illuminated the dark night, and the voices of the guests in the living room suddenly disappeared into the crevices of the eighteenth-century canopy bed as if they were never there.

It was the diplomat's wife, Angeline, who initiated the dance. She was the one who took Sir's hand into her own and guided him to the servants' quarters. She knew the servants were in the main house and had no reason to return to the quarters until the entire function was over and the guests had left the main house and everything was washed and cleaned and swept and dried and put away so that the house had the immaculate appearance it was so used to – a standard she herself insisted the servants maintained after every function. And tonight would be no different, she thought, as she led the man with the Lucky Strike breath into the dark, dark quarters.

A week after they danced in the dark servants' quarters, Sir started receiving calls at the office. It's the High Commissioner's Office again! Tell them I'm out! But madam insists! She says your visa has been approved, Sir. He picks up the phone reluctantly, trying to suppress the fury in his voice. They had had an agreement after the dance that night. There would be no phone calls, no contact at all. She was the one who had insisted on it! He was about to tell her this when he picked up the phone. He was about to remind her. She should know where she is, how to behave. This is a small fucking place for Christ's sake!

Manu, it's Angel. I need you. Fred left last night – bankers' convention in Singapore. He's gone for a month. It's fucking lonely up here. And the damned bats scare me, and the constant howling of dogs at night. I'm going crazy up here, Manu. I don't know what to do. I woke up this morning, and you were the first thing on my mind, darling. I need you, Manu. I really need you here right now, right this instant. I'll send down Johnny to get you, if you wish. I'll do whatever needs to be done to get you up here. I know I'm not supposed to contact you at work, but I don't know what else to do, darling. I just want you; that's all. And if I don't have you, I think I'll just jump into the valley and get eaten by wild animals.

He had his own car, of course, and did not need Johnny or anyone else to get him to wherever he needed to go. He picked up his briefcase and headed out the door. Ianeta, the secretary, was told that he was going out to his three o'clock and that he may not return. But I don't see anything on the schedule, Sir, she wanted to say but instead, nodded her head quietly and continued typing.

That afternoon the dance they performed on the eighteenth-century canopy bed was violent. So much so that when it was all over and he was gone, she found herself walking towards the bar. She picked up the telephone and started dialing. The voice on the other end responded, 'Central Police Station Apia, may I help you?'

The night is warm, and the children are singing under the ring of the moon. The sailor man with the tattoo wrapped around his arm with the naked woman walks towards the village of Obligation. He is tall and handsome, just like in her dream. He is accompanied by two other sailors, all in the same blue uniform. Their laughter is contagious. The village children laugh along with them. They ask them where the chief's house is. The shortest boy belts out another laugh and shows them to the fale in the middle of the village. The sailors throw chocolates at the children. The children search in the dark for the chocolate while the men continue to the house in the middle of the village.

She is in the back of the house, ironing, when the sailors arrive. She is shocked by their presence. She thinks of all the English words she knows and discovers what she had always known – that no matter how many she knew she did not posses the courage to use a single one of them. It is her brother Lima who runs to greet the sailors.

'Malo Sole!' he calls out.

'Howdy!' was the reply from the sailors. 'We're here to see the chief kahuna!'

'What do they want?' she calls out to her brother.

'I don't know,' her brother replies.

'We're here to talk to your dad. He's the chief, right?'

'He is not here.'

'Well, that's good. I mean, it's not good, but it's also good. Well, quite honestly, I came to see you.'

'Pardon me?'

'I saw you that first night out on the docks. You were dancing. I wanted to talk to you then, but you'd disappeared.'

'I am sorry. I do not know what to say.'

'Well, the boys and I were wondering if you could come out dancing with us tonight.'

'I am sorry. I can not go without my father's permission.'

'Oh, come on, you look like you're old enough to make your own decisions! We leave on Saturday, and it'll be great if you could come out with us tonight, just this once. I promise I'll be a true gentleman.'

'I am so sorry, Mister. I am so sorry.'

At Obligation, she is a different woman – almost a girl, even though she's twenty-seven and is the oldest woman in the village without a husband. Not to say she has not had suitors. Obligation women blame her mother's pride for it all. Why does she have to be so high and mighty? Why can't she just come down to earth and visit us once in a while? It's not like the girl is a virgin any more, right?

A virgin is a flower from heaven and a gift from the god(s) and is, therefore, a gift to us, and we must protect her. She is our pride and joy, our hopes, our dreams, our future. It is on her head that the dignity of this family is preserved. It is in her hands that the mothers of Obligation and other villages see that discipline and self-respect are foremost to the life of a girl woman and that every girl woman who is churchgoing and God-fearing is a true daughter of Obligation and makes us all proud.

She called him Blue because she saw the ocean in his eyes that first night, the night he told her she was ready for dance lessons. They were sitting on a river bank. The petals of gardenia fell from the sky and covered them both. My heart dies each time I see the colour red he had said, pressing his face into her hair. And he said it in the softest voice, his fingertips massaging her ears. I don't know what you want, Blue. But he had already turned into an eel and was making his way slowly up her thighs. When he entered the pool, her waters were warm. And at that moment, her heart opened, and a new universe rushed in to fill every pore of her body, including the tears that kept falling and falling down her face.

My Father's Stories

Tulia Thompson

In the air – the heavy, sweet smell of kerosene and smoke, the cooking spices of the woman on the corner, the salty sea breathing in and out. The sun is loud against his back. Charlie hides with his hands flat against the rough skin of the coconut palm, staying still and thin as the tree itself, a lone cowboy waiting for the shrill voice of attack. Bronco approaches. He can see him creeping, bent like a cat in his school shorts and Mack's shirt, a sulu tied around his neck like a cape.

Charlie leaps, his hands draw invisible pistols, 'Choo! Choo!' he shouts, diving into a roll. Red dust in his mouth, in his clothes, it rises like a flock of birds. Bronco is struck. He stumbles forward holding his heart. He walks in a decreasing circle. He rocks forward and back violently. Finally, he throws himself on the ground with a cry of defeat.

'Eh Bronco, is that you? Boys, is that you?' Bubu's voice calls. 'Boys, get here now. You want one hiding! Worrying me like this, you'll be late for church!' Bubu steps outside the house, balancing herself against the corrugated iron. Chickens scurry out of the way of her feet. She is wearing her church dress and pushing a handkerchief against her brow. Shell leis jostle against her chest.

'Boys!' Bubu shouts again. Mack and Earl are first. The bushes by the house start to shiver, and they climb out of them like shadows. Bronco opens his eyes and stands up slowly. Charlie lies in the red dust with his heart drumming into the ground. He imagines the ground drumming back.

The fluorescent light seems to shudder, and I blink in a small piece of the winter night. Visiting hours are officially over, and the corridor is too long with quietness. Cellophane crunches against the stems of the supermarket flowers I am carrying. The orderly signals us towards a small rectangle of yellow light coming through the glass panel of the final door.

'That's it,' he says, 'Room 6D'. I knew Dad would still be awake. I imagine him sitting up in bed with his head bent over a paperback western. Lani pushes the door open. There is an old man in a trolley bed. His skin is yellowed, his frame fragile and birdlike. He looks like the tall, thin body of a waqa pushed against storm waves. The old man is my father. I kiss his cheek and pull a plastic chair towards his bed. I sit and hold his hand. I watch myself do this orchestrated motion as if I am walking a trapeze or taking a high dive, but really my thoughts are somersaulting. Where is my father? Where is his booming voice? When did my father get old? Dad holds my hand, but his gaze is lost somewhere.

'Dad,' I say firmly, 'tell us what happened? What did you do?'

Charlie watches the light shift between the edge of the land and the sea. The land has its own aura. This is different land reaching out into the near dark. He can still hear his brothers' laughter and talanoa as they farewelled him around the grog bowl the other night. The night air had been warm with mokosoi and stories of their childhood. This is a new land of work and making money. In the darkness, the land looks sharp and cold. Charlie walks up to the captain. It is time.

'Boss,' he says, 'can I borrow a wetsuit?'

'What are you talking about?' asks the captain sternly.

'Boss,' says Charlie again, 'I need to borrow a wetsuit so I can swim into shore from here'.

'No way, Charlie, you're not getting out of work that easily. We've still got half a leg until we reach port. It's all hands on deck, mate.' The captain is a Kiwi. He looks about Charlie's age.

'Boss,' Charlie repeats, 'I'm an illegal. If we come into port here, and I'm on the yacht, you're going to be fined one big fine.'

'Oh bloody hell, Charlie,' the captain explodes. 'Talk about dropping me in the shit, mate.' He starts to laugh. 'Well, you better get your arse out of here then, you cheeky bugger. You can keep the bloody wetsuit.'

Even through the wetsuit, the water is cold. Charlie draws long strokes to carry him to shore. The sea is choppy close to land, and every so often, spray breaks over his face as he tilts his head up to breathe. The sea tastes new. Charlie pulls himself onto the shore and lies flat against the damp sand. His eyes search out the electric lights of houses that are nearby. Shapes rise towards him like spirits as he adjusts to the terrain. Later, he will learn that this is Takapuna Beach. He will return and walk this beach many times, as if searching for something.

When my father talks his hands dance around him like birds. His eyes dance. Storytelling animates him, he shape shifts like a changing spirit.

'Well,' he says, 'I knew I should have gone to sit with Aunty Mere, who had passed. I sat with her last night and Uncle and them. But today, I knew that the tree had to be cut down, so I thought I could go later in the evening. I knew that was the wrong thing to do. Something told me, go and sit with Aunty. But I thought, well, I can just cut this tree down before the weather changes.' Dad pauses, his eyes are red and tired.

'Well, I stood on the roof and cut the tree, like this see, on a diagonal like this. I thought it would fall away. Then I turned around to climb back down. Well, the tree fell back on me and pushed me down the roof. That's how my leg got cut up on the corrugated iron roof. It pushed me off the roof.'

My sister is exasperated. 'Don't you think, Dad, that it wasn't a very safe thing to do?'

'Io, dear,' says Dad emptily. 'But I cut away like this so the tree would fall the other way. But I tell you something, I should have gone and sat with your Aunty Mere.'

'Don't you think, Dad,' says my sister again more loudly, 'that it wasn't very safe to cut a tree down while standing on a roof?' My sister, she's a lawyer.

'What happened next, Dad?' I coax.

'Well, I came in here, and the doctor said I needed a general so that they could sew up all the layers. There's all layers of muscle and tissue they needed to sew up. And my other foot, where I landed, all my toes had been pushed into my foot. They had to pop my toes out.'

'In, right into your foot, Dad?' I say.

'Io, daughter,' says my father, 'and they popped them right back out. It's incredible what they can do.'

Charlie is in his thirties, nearly the same age as his dad when he died. He could remember thinking his father was an old man. It's a Saturday morning, and he's already back from the markets where he managed to pick up some fruit and palusami from back home. The palusami was smuggled into New Zealand by an old lady. The ghetto blaster is leaning against the back step, and the Jackson Five are singing on the radio. Charlie is sitting in the garden cutting up sugar cane with his machete and handing it to his two daughters to chew and spit. Every so often, one of the elderly Pākehā women next door will put her head over the fence to find out what is going on. Or the Māori kids over the back fence will throw over some rotten apples.

'Back in Lautoka,' he says to the girls, 'we could have sugar cane all the time. There were big fields of it. All of it was going to the sugar cane factory. That's where your grandparents worked – my dad and mum. Now, when I was only as big as you, my brothers and I loved playing cowboys. That was our favorite game because we used to go and see the cowboy pictures at the picture theatre. We wanted so much to be like the Americans. We used to get in so much trouble.'

A nurse appears in the doorway. 'I'm sorry, but you will need to leave soon. Your father needs his rest.'

'Dad,' I say, 'it's not okay that we only found out about the accident because Aunty Ruth called her niece Luisa and Luisa called me. We need to know from you if anything like this happens.'

'Io, I didn't want to worry you. I knew you would worry. I was going to tell you when I got home from the hospital. I don't know how your Aunty Ruth found out. She only found out because she called around right when it happened.'

'Dad,' I tease 'it's embarrassing when we have all the family calling like that, and we don't even know what is going on! You know how that coconut wireless works with the Fiji crew! We are your daughters.'

Dad chuckles. 'I know you're my daughters. Of course I know that! In fact, did I ever tell you the story about when I first found out about you, I was sure you were going to be boys because boys run in the family. My father had six sons, eh? So I named you both after my brothers. I told everyone, sarenga! I'm having twin sons. Then when you were born, I fainted in the hospital room. I was so nervous I had to wait outside. The nurse came out and said, "You have two lovely daughters!" I was so shocked that my sons were actually daughters!'

The nurse appears again in the doorway. We get up to leave. I kiss Dad on the cheek and whisper 'Moce'. This time, the corridor is dark apart from a bluish night light hanging at the end, like a lighthouse alone in the dark sea.

I leave my father to sleep. The night is so clear and cold that the stars are icicles. At home, I make a cup of sweet tea and cry into sleep. I dream of an old marama leaning back bent over a fine mat. She is weaving and softly singing 'Isa Lei'. At some point in the dream

I realise that the strands she is weaving are the stories my father has told me. The strands are laughing and singing, swimming or eating sugar cane. The strands are my own life, shifting versions of myself, shifting versions of the family around me. The strands weave the distance between New Zealand and Fiji, stories of going home and stories of arriving. At some point, like a pair of graceful hands becoming birds, like a spirit changing form, my father's stories became part of my own.

The Authors

Afshana Ali is a recent migrant from Fiji who is currently working at Auckland University of Technology. She is a bonafide bookworm and history buff. At the moment, she is attempting to write her first novel about being a female migrant struggling with two cultures and attempting to make sense of love, family and marriage, Indo-Fijian style!

Tusiata Avia is a New Zealand Samoan poet, writer and performer. Her first book of poetry, *Wild Dogs Under My Skirt*, was published in 2004 to critical acclaim and was shortlisted for the 2006 Prize in Modern Letters. She is currently working on a new book.

Chris Baker (Samoan/Celtic), a former environmental campaigner, is currently pursuing a BA (majoring in English) at Otago University. He also lectures medical students on the psychological implications of disability and is particularly concerned with manifestations of institutional racism, rife among the teaching staff, and is constantly in trouble for rattling the bars of the academic cage.

Taria Baquié was born in Rarotonga, Cook Islands. Her mother is Cook Island Māori and her father is Australian. She has lived in New Zealand for most of her life and is currently studying at the University of Auckland.

Cherie (Serie) Barford was born in Aotearoa to a German-Samoan mother (Stunzner/Betham/Leaega of Lotofaga and Fulu/Jamieson of Luatuanu'u) and a palagi father. She also acknowledges

Algonquin Indian ancestry through the Jamieson line. She has worked as a school teacher and is now a community education worker in Waitakere City. Her work has been published in *Whetu Moana, Poetry NZ 32, Snorkel 1, Oban 06, BMP 13 & 16, Tinfish 16/Trout 13*. She is currently working on a poetry manuscript entitled *Tapa Talk*.

Leilani Burgoyne is a New Zealand-born 'afakasi' Samoan who was born and raised in Auckland. She recently completed a Masters degree in history at the University of Auckland and is currently working for the Ministry of Foreign Affairs and Trade. Her poetry is an expression of her identity.

Tanielu de Mollard is an Aucklander of Samoan and Pākehā descent. In 2003, he was runner-up to the Katherine Mansfield Memorial Award. He is twenty-two years old.

Naila Fanene is Samoan. On her father's side, she is a Fanene from Saleilua, Falealili. On her mother's side, her aiga is Fata and Maulolo in Afega. She has worked as an English language teacher in the Solomon Islands, Australia and New Zealand and is currently an English language lecturer at the Auckland University of Technology.

She is a self-taught writer and draws from experiences of her life as a New Zealand Samoan and those of her traditional Samoan parents and grandparents to inspire her writing. Her next project is an easy-to-follow guide for new teachers of New Zealand-born Samoan students.

Florence Faumuina-Aiono was raised in a single-parent home with Samoan and Tuvaluan heritage, and she did not receive any real exposure to her Pacific birthright. Her struggle to own her Pacific culture and her unusual upbringing clashed two strong societies – the dominance of the palagi and the pride of fa'a Samoa. Her writings reflect personal struggles and the issues and conflict faced when these worlds collide.

New Zealand-born Florence Aiono (Ms Utumalamalemele Malaefou, Savalalo, Samoa – late Mr Fonofili Faumuina, Lefaga, Samoa – late Mr Tofiga Valuaga – Tuvalu) is married to New Zealand-born David Aiono (Mr Aiono Samoa, Fasito'outa – Mrs Ivone Aiono nee Neioti, Falevao) and has three children.

Zora Feilo-Makapa is creative in the field of her passion – photography, but is willing to try different mediums. When opportunities present themselves, she believes in herself enough to give things a go. She is a New Zealand-born Niue Islander, mother to a young family, and works in the field of haematology as a medical laboratory technician.

Sia Figiel is a single parent who lives with her children in the village of Vailoa, American Samoa. She has written three novels, a poetry collection and a CD collaboration with the poet Teresia Teaiwa. Sia works as a senior administrative assistant to Congressman Faleomavaega E. F. Hunkin. She is an active power walker as well as an involved parent in her children's taekwondo, piano lessons and reading programmes.

Jason Greenwood is Samoan-born. He arrived in New Zealand with parents and siblings as an eight-year-old and lived in Wanganui for ten years before moving to Auckland. He studied drama in Sydney and worked as an actor (and other jobs) for several years before returning to New Zealand. He obtained a Masters degree in Performing and Creative Arts from the University of Auckland.

Angela Gribben lives in Auckland with her husband and child. She has a Bachelor of Commerce from the University of Auckland and is continuing to explore multiple mediums in storytelling, including writing, acting, film-making and installation.

Janice Hy-bee Lauaki Ikiua has been writing poetry since she was a little girl. She was raised in the heart of Porirua, Cannons

Creek, and her parents, family members, close friends, love life, Niue Island, travels and growing up in 'The Creek' have been a main sources of inspiration for her poems. *Pikorua* is dedicated to her late father, Sam Kakina Ikiua, and also her dear ohana who inspired this poem and live in Hawai'i.

Daren Kamali was born in Fiji and is of Fijian, Wallis and Futuna, and European descent. He has lived for seventeen years in Fiji and fifteen years in New Zealand, combining the two worlds to draw inspiration for his writing, poetry, music and everyday life.

Philomena Lee is currently doing an MA in museum and cultural heritage at the University of Auckland. She is Samoan-born and emigrated, as a child, to New Zealand with her family in the mid-1950's.

Marisa Maepu is a Samoan New Zealander, born and raised in Auckland, New Zealand. She graduated with an MA (Hons) in English literature from the University of Auckland in 2000. Marisa lives in Wellington with her husband and currently works as a policy analyst for the Ministry of Health. She is an aspiring fiction writer and enjoys writing from a New Zealand-born Samoan perspective.

Selina Tusitala Marsh is of Samoan, Tuvalu and New Zealand descent. Passionate about writing, particularly poetry, she wrote a doctoral thesis on the first five Pacific women poets to publish in English. She graduated with her PhD in 2005 and now lectures in New Zealand and Pacific Literature at the University of Auckland. She lives on Waiheke Island with David, and their three sons, Javan, Micah and Davey, and extended family members.

Karlo Mila is a New Zealand-born Pacific poet of Tongan, palangi and Samoan heritage. Karlo has had a book of poems published by Huia, titled *Dream Fish Floating*. She was raised in Palmerston North but now lives in Auckland with her husband and two sons.

She is currently a PhD student at Massey University and juggles writing, academia, contract work and a young family.

Noelle Moa is happily married and a mother of two beautiful little boys. Hailing from Auckland, she is currently residing in Sydney with her aiga and working in the arts sector, but she maintains a firm loyalty to Aotearoa. Her background is in the visual arts, though she is an aspiring writer. She is currently working on a play.

Tim Page comes from a background in commercial television. Like most New Zealanders, he is of mixed descent - English, Tongan and Danish are the ones he knows about. Tim is a graduate of the University of Auckland, where he currently works. He is married to Sue, and they have two children. Tim is also a musician, and has released two albums of original songs.

Douglas Poole was born in 1970 and is of Samoan and English descent. He edits and publishes the online poetry journal *Blackmail Press*. He lives with his beautiful aiga, wife, Anja, and three children, Jarah, Waipapa and Parone-Vincent, in Waitakere City, Auckland.

Priscilla Rasmussen was born to Samoan parents. Her father's family is from Fuluasou in Lepea, Upolu and her mother's family is from Savalalo, and Iva in Sava'i. She grew up in Wellington but has lived in Samoa and South Korea. Priscilla's background is in journalism and television production, and she is currently working on a book that includes the chapter in *Niu Voices*.

Philip Siataga is of Samoan and New Zealand European heritage and is the very proud father of two wonderful daughters. Philip gained a BA in community and family studies, a Diploma for Graduates in theology and a Postgraduate Diploma in education from the University of Otago. A former social worker and counsellor, Philip currently works as a freelance researcher focusing on the mental health and social well-being of Pacific peoples. He is working on several stories and completed his first film script, *Blowing Kisses*, in 2005. That year, he was runner-up in the Huia and *Spasifik* short fiction competition for his story *The Mud House*.

Eric Smith attained a Bachelor's Degree in Fine Arts in 2000. He works as a magazine designer for an Auckland production company and lives by St Lukes with his wife Natalia. He is co-writing a play while organising other projects, including the production of For The Love of Lia as a short film. This short story draws on experiences in Samoa, where his family lived for three years while his father, Fiu, fulfilled a building contract in the early eighties.

Rev Mua Strickson-Pua is married to Linda and has a daughter Ejay and a son Feleti and is Papa to Jane Filemu, Che'den Sofi and Dremayer Liberty Choir. His background is in theology and community development. He is also a poet, storyteller, comedian, rapper, artist, dancer and photographer. He writes and performs Soc Doco Poetry, which focuses on the structure of society and its impact on people and the larger ramifications of everyday things.

Elenoa Tamani is a high school English teacher. She majored in English, history and politics at the University of the South Pacific. She enjoys writing as a hobby, but reading is her passion.

Aaron Taouma has a background in teaching, the arts, television and film work. He enjoys writing, music, film and literature, and so it is natural to create in these media. A father of three, Aaron would love one day to be able to produce that all elusive novel or screenplay.

Teresia Teaiwa is of Banaban, I-Kiribati and African-American heritage. She was born in Honolulu, Hawai'i, raised in the Fiji Islands and lives in Wellington, New Zealand. Teresia has one published collection of poetry, *Searching for Nei Nim'anoa*, and her writing has featured in a number of places, including the spoken word CD, *TERENESIA: Amplified Poetry and Songs by Teresia Teaiwa and Sia Figiel.*

Tulia Thompson is a New Zealand-born Pacific woman of mixed Fijian, Tongan and Pākehā descent. She is currently completing her doctoral degree in sociology at the University of Auckland. She is also writing a children's novel, *Josefa and the Vu*, which will be published by Huia Publishers.

Christina Tuapola was born and raised in the garden city of Christchurch, Aotearoa New Zealand. Her heritage goes back to the centre of the Pacific – the wonderful islands of Samoa. She attributes her inspiration and creativity to the backbone of her inner core – her wonderfully patient and supportive aiga. The story in this anthology is for her aiga.

Afterword

Coconuts don't grow in Aotearoa New Zealand – botanically speaking that is. But as this collection of niu/new voices attests, they do. They've been flourishing in this comparatively milder climate since the first major influx of Pacific peoples in the 1950s. As the political and social climate has changed, so have the meanings associated with niu or coconut. It has gone from being a largely descriptive word pre-1960s, to a highly derogatory one in the 1970s and 1980s, to inflecting a proud indigeneity to the Pacific in the 1990s and beyond. In literature, Aotearoa New Zealand has progressively begun to creatively acknowledge its position in the Pacific, and its many Pacific peoples are increasingly making known the fact that it is anchored in moana niu a kiwa, the Great Ocean of Kiwa.

Niu, the life giving nut for many Pacific nations, has in our context of Aotearoa New Zealand, become symbolic of many life-giving attributes that grow here, but are rooted in island soils. These Pacific influences flavour the juices of creativity, strengthen the fibre of Pacific cultures and customs as they are lived in this relatively new/niu context. While there are common themes in this collection that are comparable with Pacific literature as a genre, the meat from the nut is definitely infused with local tastes and flavours. This makes it different from the Fiji based anthology published by the Niu Wave Writers' Collective established in 1995 and of which Teaiwa (*Real Natives Talk About Love*) was a co-ordinator. *Niu Waves: Contemporary Writing from the Pacific* (2001) is a related but different species, respectfully acknowledged here.

Several thematic strands become quickly apparent in *Niu Voices*. One is the primacy of family in storytelling: great grandparents, grandparents, parents, other relatives, and siblings form the central stem for stories by Baquié, Thompson, Rasmussen, Moa, Fanene, Taouma, and Poole. They are set in the home, on the street, in hospital and in memory. Those who have gone before us become the 'stories within us' to paraphrase Barford.

Another strand developed by this emerging niu generation of writers is the constant negotiation (or what Burgoyne refers to as 'navigating' in *Brown Soul*) needed by characters who occupy what Wendt acknowledged as the 'va' in his seminal paper on Pacific literature[1], that space in between ourselves and others, ourselves and the world. This includes the ever-widening cultural and social spaces between Aotearoa born/bred children and the ways of their Island-based parents. Some characters are adept 'borderlanders'[2], successfully occupying the margins of several different, sometimes diametrically opposed cultural borders. We see this humorously negotiated in Tuapola's *Bifobology* where she theorises about cultural difference and distinctiveness by using the family as a microcosm for wider Samoan society. This is also evident in works about being afakasi where identities are conscientiously (Marsh's *Afakasi pours herself afa cuppa coffee*) and mischievously (Mila's *An educated perspective*) forged.

These negotiations are inherent in the wider thematic exploration of the Pacific diaspora and the psychological voyaging and exploration of those who have settled here. To revisit the circumstances surrounding migration, is to also revisit the hardships and sacrifices endured to come to Aotearoa New Zealand. Many works are a creative inventory of what was lost and gained in journeying to Wellington (Rasmussen's *The Return*, Otago (Siataga's *Fugue*), or Auckland (Fanene's *Eti's Dilemma*) or even back 'home' to the Islands (Smith's *For the Love of Lia* or

---

[1] See 'Tatauing the Post-Colonial Body' *Inside Out: Literature, Cultural Politics, and Identity in the New Pacific*, Vilsoni Hereniko and Rob Wilson, Rowman & Littlefield, 1999, 399-412.
[2] A term popularised by Chicana feminist Gloria Anzaldua in her first book *Borderlands/La Frontiera: The New Mestiza*. San Francisco: Aunt Lute Books, 1987.

Faumuina-Aiono's *The Risky Journey to Belong*). Such psychological navigations towards that ever-elusive notion of home is epitomised in Kamali's succinct *Pacific Migration* when a boy 'gazes on an Island map stuck to his wall' and reminisces about village life. He eventually concludes, as must we all, that he 'takes his home wherever he goes'.

Other journeys exist in traversing difference on social and cultural terrain. We read of characters endeavouring to make connections, holistically and genealogically (Barford's *Connections*) and in the humdrum of daily realilty (Page's *Bus*). But life itself is the journey. People pack their cargo of culture with them, along with their preconceived ideas about where they are going. The unexpected occurs when they realise that their cargo transforms, mutates, and metamorphosises along the way, as seen in Avia's poem where Nafanua evades the religious police. In Maepu's *A Requiem for a Dream*, R. L. Stevenson takes Ana on numerous dream-dates. She is chosen to finish his famously unfinished, and arguably finest, work. Which begs the question: what would the famous Scottish writer's story look like if finished off by a Pacific woman? Culture has always been in flux. Always will be.

Maybe it's because we like cowboy movies. If cowboy movies could be a theme in itself, then I'd pick that as another ever-present strand in Pacific literature. What belies its popularity is Pacific identification with certain aspects of popular culture: in this instance, the heroism, the overcoming of hardship, the humour, the conquering of the colonial frontier – in reverse! It's like that popular joke told about the moment Zorro finds himself surrounded by Indians and says to his partner: 'C'mon, we better get out of here!' To which Tonto replies: 'What do you mean "we", white man?'[3] It's an appreciation of life through humour in all its forms: from the dry and understated humour of Baquié, to the loud, raucous comedy of Taouma, to the irreverent, side-

---

[3] See also Haunani-Kay Trask's essay 'What Do You Mean "We", White Man?' in *From a Native Daughter: Colonialism and Sovereignty in Hawai'i*. Honolulu: University of Hawai'i Press, 1993.

splitting, satirical comedy in Baker's *No Sex Please, We're Disabled*. Often underlining such humour is a sober reality faced by those on the borders, the colonial frontiers as seen in Figiel's exploration of the sexual politics of Island life and its colonial remnants in *The Dancers*, or Greenwood's *Palauli*, or any one of the stories problematising religion (Lee), relationships (Teaiwa, de Mollard), success (Gribben, Ali and Tamani, Pua), and home (Feilo-Makapa, Ikiua).

This collection of niu voices offers creative sustenance from a new generation of writers emerging from the Pacific diaspora in Aotearoa New Zealand. Climb. Pluck. Pierce. Drink.

Selina Tusitala Marsh
Editor *Niu Voices*